Dani had rehearsed the speech so many times that even she was beginning to believe it. "It's as if you're supposed to do this. While we don't know who gave you the money for a wish, I think you should use it to get something you've always wanted. Listen, even a trillion dollars can't make you well, but the money you've gotten *can* help you have some fun. I say let's go for it! You deserve to see the ocean, whether Mom agrees or not. I'm going to help you make your wish come true."

Other Bantam Starfire Books you will enjoy

ONE LAST WISH

Lurlene McDaniel

Mourning Song

BANTAM BOOKS
NEW YORK • TORONTO • LONDON • SYDNEY • AUCKLAND

RL 5, age 10 and up

MOURNING SONG

A Bantam Book/May 1992

The Starfire logo is a registered trademark of Bantam Books, a division of
Bantam Doubleday Dell Publishing Group, Inc.
Registered in U.S. Patent and Trademark Office and elsewhere.

ISBN 0-553-29810-0

Published simultaneously in the United States and Canada

Bantam Books are published by Bantam Books, a division of Bantam
Doubleday Dell Publishing Group, Inc. Its trademark, consisting of the
words "Bantam Books" and the portrayal of a rooster, is Registered in
U.S. Patent and Trademark Office and in other countries. Marca Reg-
istrada. Bantam Books, 666 Fifth Avenue, New York, New York 10103.

PRINTED IN THE UNITED STATES OF AMERICA

RAD 0 9 8 7 6 5 4 3

Mourning Song

One

"I DON'T BELIEVE you." Dani Vanoy's voice shook with anger and disbelief.

"I wouldn't lie to you or your mother, Dani," Dr. Phillips answered sadly. "Surely you know that by now."

Dani glanced at her mother, sitting beside her in the hospital conference room. She wanted her mother to challenge Dr. Phillips and deny what Dani didn't want to accept. Her mother's face was chalky white and her voice shook as she asked, "Are you absolutely certain?"

"Cassie's tumor is malignant and inoperable.

We can't cut it out without killing her," Dr. Phillips explained. "I'm sorry."

Dani felt hot and cold, and sick to her stomach. Her sister, Cassie, was only seventeen, just two years older. How could she be dying? Cassie's problems had started with headaches four months before, in January. The headaches had grown worse. Dani recalled how her sister used to lie on her bed and weep from the pain. Their family doctor, Dr. Cody, had diagnosed migraines and prescribed medication, but the drugs left Cassie feeling no better. The pain persisted.

Then, a few weeks ago, Cassie lost some feeling on her left side. Her eyelid drooped, she stumbled trying to walk, and her speech slurred. She became so dizzy, she couldn't stand up. Dr. Cody recommended a neurologist, and Mom had taken Cassie to Dr. Nathan Phillips, whom it turned out she had dated in college.

Having Cassie's condition diagnosed and placing her under the care of an old friend had given Dani's mom some peace of mind. Dani had spent the last few weeks in a state of panic. How could her sister have headaches one day and then suddenly be totally incapacitated the next? Dr. Phillips had checked Cassie into the hospital. After a series of CAT scans, MRI X rays, and countless other tests, he revealed the results. Cassie had a brain tumor that could not be removed.

"So, if you cut it out, it kills her. And if you leave it alone, it kills her," Dani said bitterly. "Some choice."

"Isn't there anything to be done?" Mrs. Vanoy asked.

"I'll start her on radiation and chemo immediately, but I'll be honest—this kind of tumor has a poor response to treatment."

"What about that gamma knife radiation surgery you told Mom and me about?"

Dr. Phillips's face looked weary. "Cassie's tumor is located so deep inside her brain and so close to her brain stem that we cannot risk gamma knife surgery."

"There must be something you can do, Nathan." Dani's mother's voice was so soft, so desperate that Dani felt chilled to the bone.

Dr. Phillips reached out and took her mother's hand. "Catherine, this is the toughest moment in a doctor's professional life. To have to look at a patient's family and say, 'There's nothing I can do.' I'm supposed to be a healer—a fixer of the human body. I'm not supposed to be telling you that I feel helpless and defeated, but I do, and I am."

Dani felt tears well in her eyes. Dr. Phillips's honesty, the catch in his voice as he'd spoken left her with little doubt. Medical science had done everything it could for her sister. Dani recognized death staring at them. She'd seen it once before, when she'd been six, when her father, a policeman, had been killed in the line of duty. She remembered being told that Daddy wasn't ever coming home again. She'd been overwhelmed with grief and fear, but eventually had realized her mother and sister were still there for her. Now, Cassie was being taken, too. It wasn't fair. She began to tremble.

"At the very best, all we can do is retard the tumor's growth," Dr. Phillips continued.

"That will give her more time," Dani's mother said eagerly.

"How much more?" Dani asked.

"Maybe a month or two," the doctor said.

"Is that all? What kind of help is that?" Dani's voice was full of anger.

"Every hour she *has* is a help," her mother declared. "Who knows, maybe Nathan will think of something else to try. Maybe some new drug or surgical technique will come along. As far as I'm concerned, time means hope."

Dr. Phillips was still holding Dani's mother's hand. Her mom looked up and asked, "Will we be able to bring Cassie home again?"

"Yes, but not until she finishes up initial radiation and chemo." Dr. Phillips paused as if to choose his next words carefully. "Once she returns home, it won't be easy for the two of you to care for her by yourselves. Of course, there's Cincinnati's hospice group. Or if you want, you can hire a private-duty nurse."

"I can take care of my sister," Dani was insistent. In less than three weeks, school would be out for the summer, and she could stay with Cassie full-time.

Her mother nodded. "Dani and I can handle it. My boss understands, and he'll let me work flexible hours. We want to do this for Cassie. I don't want strangers caring for her."

"As the tumor grows, she'll experience some severe symptoms," Dr. Phillips said, his voice level and professional. "She'll lose her faculties, her memory. She may go blind. As she deteriorates, you'll have to have help with her. The hospice people are professionally trained and very caring, very sensitive."

"If she starts downhill, I'll bring her right back to the hospital," Mom replied. "But as long as we can keep her at home, we will."

Dani tried to tune out the doctor's voice. She wanted to detach herself from the conversation. If only she could pretend that she was watching a TV show, that it was some make-believe character they were talking about and not her sister. "She should know, Mom. You should tell Cassie she's going to die."

"No." Her mother's expression looked determined. "She doesn't need this burden while she's going through all the therapies. Dani, you must promise me you won't tell her, or even hint that we know her chances are so slim. Please, Dani, promise me."

Dr. Phillips interrupted. "Catherine, it might be wisest to level with Cassie. She's not a little kid. Sooner or later, she'll surmise the truth."

Dani's mother shook her head stubbornly. "When she has to know, I'll tell her. But as long as she's in treatment, I don't want her told."

"But, Mom—"

"No." She cut off Dani's protest. "Positive mental attitude is important—that's a fact. If she thinks the treatments are useless, then she really will have no chance."

Dani understood her mother's point of view, but still thought she was wrong. Dani was certain Cassie would want to know. She realized that now wasn't the time to try and persuade her mother to level with Cassie.

"Now, you'll promise me?" her mother asked.

"I promise not to tell her," Dani said.

"Not even a hint of negativity."

"Not a hint." Dani pressed her lips together and rose. The room had grown stuffy. "I want to go see Cassie now. She's expecting me."

Her mom reached out for her, and Dani slipped into her arms. They clung tightly for a moment. "Tell her I'll be up in a while. I want to talk more with Dr. Phillips."

Dani nodded, her throat so clogged with tears that she couldn't speak. She left the conference room and stepped into the busy flow of medical personnel hurrying through the halls. She spun, slipped into a bathroom, and started sobbing. The doctor's news hit her hard. She hadn't expected anything so hopeless. Obviously, Dr. Phillips cared for Cassie. He seemed to care for their mother, too. But still, he was only human—only a doctor with limitations. Dani washed her face and tried to pull herself together. She had to go face her sister with no hint of negativity.

Two

As DANI NEARED her sister's room, she heard excited giggles and realized some of Cassie's friends from school were visiting. Dani leaned against the wall outside the room and waited. She heard their chatter about the trip Cassie's senior class had just made to Florida and felt even sorrier for her sister. Since Disney World, Cape Canaveral, and the beach were only twenty hours away from Cincinnati, it had been the perfect choice for Westview High's senior class. Cassie had primed their mother about her going ever since she'd been a junior, but she'd been in the hospital when the class had left.

Dani overheard Angela give details of some hunk she met on the beach, and someone else described the fun they'd had. Dani hoped they weren't tiring Cassie.

Once the girls were gone, Dani went in. She found Cassie propped up in bed, crying. "What's wrong?"

"My friends were telling me about the senior trip and how much fun they had." Cassie shrugged miserably. Large, dark circles smudged the fragile skin beneath her brown eyes. Her once long chestnut-color hair had been shaved off for the biopsy. Cassie looked small and vulnerable, like a shorn, helpless lamb. On her bed was a bag from Disney World.

Dani sat on the edge of the bed. "Can I peek?" Cassie nodded, and Dani sorted through the items. There was a stuffed Mickey Mouse toy; a T-shirt that read, "My friends went to Florida, and all I got was this lousy shirt"; and a glass jar full of seawater, sand, and assorted shells. She didn't know whether to be glad or angry for Cassie's sake. On the one hand, the gifts only magnified her sister's sadness over not going, but on the other, it was gratifying to know at least her friends had remembered her.

"There's this, too," Cassie said. "It's a conch shell." She lifted a large shell that was curled and pointed on one end with a brilliant pink cast that shone with a pearl-like luster in the light.

Dani took it. "Hold it to your ear," Cassie told her. "You can hear the sound of the sea."

Dani did, and she heard something that sounded like hollow static. She grinned. "That's neat."

"I know." Cassie covered her face with her hands. "I wanted to go so much."

Dani wished she had some brilliant words of comfort for Cassie, but she didn't. She put the shell down on the bed and gave her sister a hug.

Cassie reached for some tissues. "Where's Mom?" she asked.

"She'll be up soon. She had to take care of something." Dani purposefully didn't look her sister in the eye.

"Don't let Mom know I was crying. It seems so dumb to be upset about the trip when I'm stuck in the hospital with all these tests. All my life I've dreamed about walking the beach and swimming in the waves. It seems like such a small thing to want to see the ocean. Why is this medical mess happening to me?"

"I wish you could've gone, too, Cassie. Maybe later this summer." Dani could hardly keep her voice from breaking as she spoke. Cassie would probably be dead before summer was over.

Cassie blew her nose. "So, tell me." She smiled,

obviously trying to change the subject, "What's going on at school?"

"I have a research paper due soon. I don't know what to write about," Dani answered glumly. "At this rate, I'll never pass tenth grade."

"Why don't you do your paper on brain tumors? I'll help you. I'm becoming an expert."

"I think that's a bad joke. You shouldn't talk like that," Dani said.

"If I don't joke, I'll cry," Cassie replied.

Dani felt like crying, too, but knew she had to keep up a cheerful front for Cassie's sake and because she'd promised her mom.

"Are you cold?" Cassie asked. "You're shivering."

"I'm fine. Listen, do you want to watch TV?" Without waiting for an answer, Dani fumbled with the remote control device and flipped on the television braced high in the ceiling corner. A nature program was on, and Dani groaned inwardly. She tried to change the channel as the voice and scene talked about the sea.

"Wait," Cassie said. "Don't change the channel. Let's watch. Perfect timing. We were just talking about the ocean."

It was a documentary about loggerhead turtles. The host of the show was explaining how the turtles were threatened by extinction because their beachfront nesting sites were being turned into high-rise buildings and condos.

"This is boring," Dani protested, trying to take her sister's attention off the subject.

"I want to watch," Cassie said. Dani resigned herself to watching the program. She only half listened to the plight of the baby turtles as they hatched from buried nests and rushed toward the water and survival. The announcer explained that the turtles were naturally drawn by the light of the moon and stars, but now the glow of artificial lights was sending them instead onto parking lots and highways or into the reach of waiting predators.

"Poor turtles," Cassie mumbled. "I feel sorry for them."

"They're only turtles," Dani said, wishing Cassie would save her pity for herself.

"They're victims," Cassie insisted, and her gaze met Dani's and held it.

Dani felt her chest tighten. Victims. *Like you.* The tumor is victimizing you—draining away your life while everyone stands by helplessly.

There was hope for those turtles. For Cassie, there was nothing to be done.

Three

"Why have you been avoiding me all day, Dani?" Austin Cole asked.

Dani jumped. She thought she'd hidden herself from the prying eyes and questions of classmates in the school library. "I've got a paper to write," she mumbled.

Austin placed his hands on each side of her open notebook. "I've been watching you. You've been staring into space ever since you got here." Dani looked up at him.

"You have no right to spy on me," she snapped. She didn't even know why she was angry at Austin, but she didn't want to apologize.

"Friends don't shut friends out," Austin said gently.

Austin piled up her books. "Come on. Let's get out of here."

"Hey, wait—give me my books. I don't want to leave."

Austin ignored her and started walking. Dani quickly followed him outside to the parking lot, where he opened the door of his car. He motioned for her to get in. Dani made a face.

"Don't be stubborn," Austin warned. "Just get in before I take off with your books."

With a toss of her red hair, Dani climbed in. Austin settled in the driver's seat, shoved the car into gear, and headed out away from school.

Dani and Austin had been friends almost since the first day they'd met. She wasn't sure how Austin always seemed to pick up on her feelings, but he did.

In a high school where money, brains, and beauty counted most, Dani felt poor, dumb, and ugly. Her red hair, fair complexion, and green-brown eyes made her look the opposite of her sister, Cassie. Cassie never seemed to feel out of it, despite the family's having to struggle to keep up.

Good grades didn't come easily to Dani, even though she studied hard. Dani was athletic. She preferred sports to academics, and realized early on that her meager baby-sitting earnings didn't go far toward buying designer clothes worn by most of the girls at Westview. Dani didn't find much to recommend about her high school experience.

Austin, who'd moved to Cincinnati the year before, had entered Westview High midterm. He'd gone to so many schools growing up, he had been placed with Dani's class even though he was seventeen and technically a junior. Austin's parents were missionaries who were now associated with the church Dani and her mother and sister regularly attended. Austin spoke several languages, wore his blond hair in a ponytail, had sky blue eyes, and was good-looking. Dani wasn't interested in Austin as a boyfriend, really. But she liked having a friend who was a boy.

Austin glanced toward Dani. "Okay ... so, I shouldn't have kidnapped you. But, you avoided me all day, and I figured something's wrong. What's up?"

"Nothing's wrong. I told you, I have a paper due." She wasn't ready to spill to anybody what was going on with Cassie. She couldn't bear to actually say the words.

"How about playing racquetball with me? I'll spot you two points."

At the town house complex where Austin lived, there was a recreation area. He and Dani often played. His suggestion sounded good. She wanted to smash something. "You're on, wise guy. And

forget the points. I can take you without the char-
ity."

"My rackets are in the trunk. After I stomp you,
you can come over, and I'll make you one of my
famous OJ specials."

When they arrived at the outdoor racquetball
courts, the afternoon sun and concrete walls were
making angular shadows across the courts. Dani
swung the racket and bounced on the balls of her
feet to warm up. She served, propelling the ball in
a power shot.

"Okay, hot shot, no more Mr. Nice Guy," Austin called. He followed up his taunt with a wicked
shot that whizzed past her racket like a bullet.
With determination, Dani buckled down to win
the game.

They played for forty minutes. Dani was soaked
with perspiration, and her hands felt numb from
holding the racket. Her breath came hard, and her
muscles ached, but she felt exhilarated and almost free of the terrible feeling that had been
weighing her down emotionally for two days.

"I give up!" Austin finally yelled. "You're killing
me, girl." He collapsed on the court, where he lay
panting, spread-eagle.

Dani scooped up the ball and sat down on the
hard concrete. Her legs felt rubbery, and her heart
was pounding, but she gave him a satisfied smirk.
"Wimp!" she gibed.

"I didn't think I was taking on the bionic woman," Austin gasped. He sat up and flashed her a sweaty grin. "So, do you feel better now?"

She stood up, not wanting to give him any satisfaction. "You promised me an OJ special. Pay up."

"I never go back on a promise." They went over to his family's town house, and he unlocked the door and led her inside. "Mom and Dad must still be up at the church," he said, stooping to scratch the head of the terrier that greeted them enthusiastically.

Dani followed Austin down the hall, dodging the frolicking dog. "I can't stay long. Right after dinner, Mom and I are going over to visit Cassie." The mention of her sister brought back the heaviness instantly. She'd been so focused on the game that for a little while, she'd forgotten.

In the kitchen, Austin started pulling out the blender and the ingredients for his concoction. Dani sat at the table and watched. The room felt overly warm. She stared up at an African mask that glared down ominously from the soffit. She looked around at the objects the Coles had obviously picked up on their travels all over the world.

Minutes later, the blender stopped whirling, and Austin served her a frothy mixture. She sipped it, still staring at the mask. Austin followed her line of vision. "That mask was a gift from a tribal medicine man in Africa. It's supposed to ward off evil spirits."

"Maybe I should borrow it for my sister."

"She's got to be in better hands than that."

"I don't think so. I'll bet that old witch doctor knows more than Cassie's doctors right now."

"You want to tell me about it?"

Haltingly, at first, she poured out her feelings of helplessness and frustration. She didn't want to cry like a baby, not even in front of Austin, but the burden of knowing her sister was going to die felt too big to handle.

"I'm really sorry, Dani," Austin said gently as he wiped her tears. "Is there anything I can do?"

She shook her head. "According to Dr. Phillips, there's nothing anyone can do. He's obviously doing all he can—it turns out he's an old friend of my mother's."

"Your mother doesn't think Cassie should know the truth?"

"Right, but I disagree with her. I think Cassie has a right to know."

He leaned back in his chair, his blue eyes serious and thoughtful. "Maybe not. Sometimes a positive mental attitude *is* a big boost."

"I would want to know. Wouldn't you?"

He shrugged. "Sometimes hope is all a person has. Why take it away?"

"But won't it hurt more if she does learn the truth? Won't she feel that we betrayed her?"

"Is that what you're afraid of? That she'll hate you because you tried to protect her from the truth?"

She *was* afraid Cassie would hate her and Mom. She couldn't bare living the rest of her life thinking Cassie had died hating her. "Yes." Dani hung her head miserably and stared down at her empty hands. "I don't want her to die. It's not fair."

"You can't stop it from happening."

His honest statement only made her angry and depressed. What kind of a universe was it if a wonderful girl had to die at seventeen? "So, what should I do while I wait for it to happen?"

"Let her know you love her, I guess. Be there for her if she needs anything. I'll do anything I can to help you."

"Will you? I feel as if I should do something more, but I don't know what."

"If you think of something, I'll help you. I promise."

She raised her glass and clinked it against his. "It's a deal."

Four

⌒∽⌒

THAT EVENING, WHEN Dani and her mom went to visit Cassie, they found her vomiting. She was running a low-grade fever, as well. "A side effect of her treatments," Dr. Phillips told them as they waited outside in the hall for the nurses to change Cassie's bed linen.

Dani's mom wrung her hands. "I can't stand having her so sick."

"I know," Dr. Phillips said kindly.

"But if it won't really help her, why are you making her go through this?" Dani blurted out.

"There's always the outside chance that her tumor will respond. We have to try," her mother answered before the doctor.

Dani felt angry with her mother. Why was her mom insisting Cassie go through such useless torture? She heard Dr. Phillips's voice. "Listen, Catherine," he was saying. "The next few weeks aren't going to be easy on any of you, but I'm throwing everything in our medical arsenal at this growth. Who knows? Maybe we'll get lucky."

As the nurses left the room, Dr. Phillips told Dani and her mom they could go in. Dani watched him give her mother's hand a squeeze. "If you need me, please call anytime—day or night."

"Thank you, Nathan. You've been a real friend."

He cleared his throat and stepped aside. Dani followed her mother into Cassie's room.

Cassie lay on the clean white sheets, her face looking pinched and wan. Her eyelids fluttered open. "Hi, Mama."

Mrs. Vanoy leaned down and kissed her. "Hi, baby."

Dani hugged her sister and felt the thinness of her body through her nightgown.

"Sorry you had to wait to see me." Cassie closed her eyes, and Dani saw a tear trickle from one corner. "Oh, Mom, I'm so sick. I can't keep anything down. They told me it's the radiation and the chemo. I hate it. I want to go home and go back to school," she said.

"You will," her mom assured her, although Dani knew it was an empty promise. "Maybe I should spend the night."

"Mom, I'm not a baby," Cassie objected. "I'll be all right."

Watching Cassie's face allowed Dani to see that her protest was halfhearted. Cassie might not want her mother sacked out in a cot next to her bed, but she obviously didn't want to be alone, either. "Let me stay," Dani begged. "I'd like to stay with Cassie."

Her mother studied Dani. "What about school tomorrow?"

"It's Memorial Day, remember? No school."

"I wouldn't mind if Dani stayed," Cassie said slowly. "That would be all right. No sense in your losing a night's sleep, Mom."

Their mother gave them a tired smile. "I can take a hint. You two don't want Mom hanging around. I think Dani's staying over for the night is a good compromise. Dani can call me if you need me."

Mrs. Vanoy arranged with the nurses for Dani to stay. A cot was brought in. She bought snack food and magazines at the hospital gift shop. "The nights get really long," she told Dani. "You can read in case you can't sleep."

Dani wasn't really crazy about staying all night in the hospital, but Cassie had perked up considerably since they'd put the plan into action. When everything was set, Mrs. Vanoy hugged them both. "I'll be back first thing in the morning."

When their mother was gone, Dani wondered exactly what to do to pass the time. "Maybe there's a good oldie-goldie movie on the late show," she said to Cassie.

Before Dani could flip on the TV, Cassie whispered to her, "I've got a secret. A really big, incredible secret. I was going to tell Mom . . . it's so incredible, I don't know what to make of it. I'm not able to find the words to tell you. Here read it for yourself."

Cassie handed Dani an envelope. "What is it?"

"Open it. Read it."

Dani pulled out a sheet of what was obviously expensive-looking paper. At the top of the sheet she noticed the embossed letters: OLW. She eagerly read:

Dear Cassie,

You don't know me, but I know about you, and because I do, I want to give you a special gift. Accompanying this letter is a certified check—my gift to you, with no strings attached, to spend on anything you want. No one knows about this gift except you, and you are free to tell anyone you want.

Who I am isn't really important. What matters is that you and I have much in common. Through no fault of our own, we have endured pain and isolation and have spent many days in a hospital feeling lonely and scared. I hoped for a miracle, but most of all, I hoped for someone to truly understand what I was going through.

I can't make you live longer, I can't stop you from hurting. But I can give you one wish, as someone did for me. My wish helped me find purpose, faith, and courage.

Friendship reaches beyond time, and the true miracle is in giving, not receiving. Use my gift to fulfill your wish.

> *Your forever friend,*
> *JWC*

Attached to the letter was a check made out to Cassie Vanoy for one hundred thousand dollars and signed by a Richard Halloway, Esq. It was labeled "One Last Wish Foundation."

Dani read the amount and whistled low. "What is this? A joke, or what?"

"I don't know," Cassie whispered. "But I think it's for real."

"It looks real to me. What are you going to do with it? You haven't told anyone else?"

"You're the only one who knows about it."

"But it's so weird! Do we know anyone with the initials JWC?"

"Not that I can think of. But whoever JWC is, I believe he or she understands. That's what makes it so awesome." Cassie's eyes glowed as she spoke. "It's so much money! It's like winning the lottery."

Dani felt a twinge of jealousy toward the faceless girl who could identify so completely with Cassie and offer such an extravagant gift. *Dani* was the one who should be doing something special for her sister. "What are you going to do with it?" she asked.

"I don't know yet. I should give it to Mom to pay all my medical bills, but I want to think about it." Cassie reached for the papers with trembling fingers. "You won't tell anyone, will you?"

Another secret Dani felt obligated to keep. "Not if you don't want me to."

"I have to think about this really carefully," Cassie said. "I want to do something very special with it. Right now, I'm not sure what."

Dani chewed on her lower lip, thinking of all

the things the money could buy. And couldn't buy. It couldn't buy Cassie's health. It couldn't buy her one moment more. The value of the gift began to pale. She stared down at the envelope, feeling like a child who'd peeked inside a closet and seen all her Christmas presents before they'd been wrapped—she would still open them when the time came, but how could she feel genuine pleasure over a mound of boxes that held no surprises?

Five

"Mom, you know it's so hard on Cassie that all her friends will graduate together without her. They'll spend the summer getting ready for college. If only she'd gotten to go on the senior trip before this happened to her."

The two of them sat in the kitchen. Cassie's empty chair was beside the one that had been Dani's father's.

"That's true," her mom said with a weary sigh. "I know how much Cassie's always talked about going to the beach and Disney World. I'm really sorry now that I just didn't borrow the money one of those summers when you two were growing up. But at the time, I thought there'd always be next year."

"Maybe we could do something special together now," Dani suggested.

"What do you mean?"

"Like a vacation. I mean, what if money weren't a problem?" Ever since Cassie had shown her the check from the One Last Wish Foundation, she'd thought of little else. Cassie had gotten enough money to do something really special, almost anything she wanted to do. Since their father's death, Dani's mother had worked. Vacations had always been a luxury. Most summers, they stayed put and saved the money, or drove out to Iowa to visit their grandparents, who were now too old and ill to travel. Dani had never really minded, but Cassie had an adventurer's streak and always longed to travel.

Mom shook her head. "Money's not an issue at this point. I'd mortgage the house before I'd let money stop me from doing something for Cassie."

Dani hadn't expected this response. "So, if money's not a problem, why don't we go do something?"

Her mother put down her fork and sighed. "Dani, we can't all just pack up and take off."

"Why not?"

"Cassie's sick." Her mother was looking at Dani

as if she thought her younger daughter had suddenly forgotten that all-important point. "We can't all pile in the car and go away. Cassie needs her treatments."

"But the treatments aren't helping."

"Maybe they will."

"Cassie really hates them, you know."

"Her medical treatments aren't up to her. I'm doing what I think is best for her."

"Even Dr. Phillips doesn't think the treatments are helping. If you gave Cassie a choice, if you told her the truth, she'd say 'forget them' and come home."

"This isn't up for a vote, Dani. Don't you know how it tears me up to see her in that hospital, so sick from the drugs they're giving her? Some of those chemo drugs are pure poison, but in order to kill off the tumor, they have to be potent. I have to follow through with this. I have to feel that we're doing everything possible. I can't simply bring her home to curl up on her bed, take pain medication, and die."

"Well, I think Cassie would prefer to come home. She would want to make the best of whatever time she had left. And she wouldn't want to die in the hospital."

"She *can* come home," Mom insisted. "We're close enough to the hospital that we can get her there quickly when necessary. Besides, the hospital has all the proper equipment to sustain her if she goes into cardiac arrest, or if she stops breathing."

This thought had never crossed Dani's mind, but she found it horrifying. She'd read stories and seen TV coverage about people being hooked up to machines in order to live when there was no hope of their ever recovering. "What if that's not what Cassie wants?"

"Of course it's what she wants."

"But how can you know for sure if you won't ask her?"

"We must give her every opportunity to continue living."

"It doesn't seem like much of a way to live. *I* wouldn't want to live that way." Dani jutted her chin. "And Cassie doesn't, either."

"Well, I guarantee you, Dani, if it was you, I would take the same measures and make the same choices."

Her mother stood abruptly. She knocked the table as she did and made the dishes and flatware rattle. The sound jarred Dani's nerves. She watched as her mother began to pace across the kitchen floor.

"Do you think this is easy for me?" her mother asked. She didn't wait for a reply. "Cassie's my child. I love her. I want to keep her with me for as long as possible. Keeping her in the hospital gives us some measure of control. Even if she has to go on life support, at least she'll be alive."

Didn't the quality of Cassie's life count for anything? Dani wondered. It wasn't as if she was ever going to get well. All medical science could do for her now was prolong a life of suffering and pain.

Her mother continued to pace and talk. "I don't make these decisions lightly, Dani. The day your father died started off like any ordinary day. I got you two girls off to school, packed his lunch, and kissed him good-bye at the back door." She turned and stared at the door, now shut and chained against the night. "I still remember the smell of his aftershave and how the light caught on his badge. He said, 'See you at dinner,' and drove away.

"I never saw him alive again—never saw him again *ever*. The car crashed and burned, and all I was allowed to see of Matt was his coffin."

Dani listened, sitting so still and rigid that her back began to ache. She had known that her dad had died chasing a robbery suspect, but her mother had never discussed it with her before. And she had so few memories of him that sometimes he didn't even seem real to her. In her mind's eye, he was always the smiling man in the photograph that Mom kept on her dresser and in the special album that highlighted his police career.

Her mother snapped herself out of her reverie. "Anyway, I had no control over what happened to your father. Just as I have no control over what's going to happen to Cassie. But what I can control, I will. And keeping her on treatments, in the hospital, under close supervision, is what I plan to do."

"But going away for only a few days—"

Mom shook her head fiercely. "Not even for one day. I can't take the chance—she might take a downward turn."

"I still think you should ask her," Dani insisted.

Mom came over and tentatively reached out and touched Dani's hair. "You're so much like your dad. Once you get hold of an idea, you don't let go. He was stubborn, opinionated, bullheaded—and absolutely the most wonderful man in the world. You're wonderful too."

Her mother's expression softened as she gazed down at Dani. "I know what I'm doing, honey. I know what's best for Cassie. Please trust me."

Dani nodded, but only because she realized it was pointless to argue. She would never persuade her mother that a few more days of life for Cassie would not be nearly so welcome as a few days of the three of them doing something fun. Much more welcome than the controlled, gleaming world of hospitals and humming machines.

Six

As Dani was walking to the bus stop, she heard a horn honk. Austin pulled alongside of her in a van and called, "Hop in."

She nodded and quickly got in. "Hi. Thanks for the ride. How come you're driving the van?"

"My car's been acting up, and since Mom and Dad are heading to Haiti for three weeks on a mission trip, they said I could drive this."

"They left you totally on your own? For three weeks?"

"Dani, we've lived all over the world. This town is no big deal. There are plenty of neighbors around if I need anything. But I know how to cook, clean up, and take care of things." He flashed her a grin. "I'm an independent guy. Are you impressed, or what?"

She rolled her eyes. "It really doesn't bother you to stay alone?"

"I've been doing it for years. When I was little and my folks were preaching in the mission field, I went with them whenever I could, but as I got older, I didn't always go."

"You're lucky that you've gotten to travel so much. I've never been anyplace except my grand-parents' farm in Iowa."

"You're one up on me—I've never been to Iowa!"

"Maybe it's true, a person always wants what he doesn't have."

"Profound." Austin let out a low whistle. "You've just summed up thousands of years of the human predicament."

They rode in silence for a while. Finally, Austin asked, "So, what's the matter? Is it Cassie?"

Dani sighed. "Cassie's not going to graduate with her class. Mom asked the school board, but they said she'd missed so much school—she hasn't done much of anything academically since she got sick in January."

"That's lousy," Austin grumbled.

Dani shrugged, although she'd been furious when her mother first told her. "Mom was upset, but she didn't press the point and decided not to make a case because then Cassie might find out she's dying, and Mom doesn't want her to know it yet."

"What did your mother tell her?"

"That she could make up the work over the summer."

"And Cassie bought that?"

"The medication Cassie takes makes her spacey. She just accepted it."

"School will be out soon," Austin observed. "Maybe the summer will go better for her."

Dani longed for the end of school, but also dreaded it. Every day that passed, meant one day less for her sister. "Mom's insisting that Cassie stay on the radiation, even though it keeps her sick as a dog. She wants to continue with treatments till the bitter end."

"I guess it makes her feel like she's doing something," Austin ventured. "Sometimes doing *anything* feels better than doing nothing."

Dani realized how much it bothered her that there was nothing to do—nothing that *she* could do for her sister. A complete stranger had offered Cassie an enormous amount of money. Sure, it was Cassie's to spend, but maybe she could help Cassie figure out something worth spending it on, something only for Cassie.

Austin pulled into the parking lot and found a

space. "You getting out," Austin asked, "or are you daydreaming?"

"I hate going in there," Dani grumbled as she stared over at the school.

"Everybody's sick of school this time of the year. Just a few more weeks till summer vacation. You can make it."

"It's not that. It's so many things, but I can't discuss them now."

"What is it?"

"Well at school, it's the way kids act around me. Whenever I walk by Cassie's friends in the halls, I hear them whispering about her. It makes me angry. Even her close friends don't come by the hospital much anymore. I think it's mean and cruel. It's not as if they're going to catch her tumor. Don't they know how lonely she gets?"

"Don't be too hard on everybody," Austin said.

She whipped around, glaring at him. "How can you defend them? You've heard them talking about her—as if she were some kind of freak."

"Don't get mad at me. I'm one of the good guys, remember?"

Grudgingly, she agreed. "I'm not mad at you. Just *them*."

"Most people—especially kids—don't know how to act around someone who's really sick. No one's ever taught them."

"What do you mean?"

"I've grown up in a lot of countries," he explained. "A lot of cultures. In America, kids never think about sickness and dying. They all think they're going to live forever. You go to movies where people get blown away like dust. Then, a week later, you see the same actor walking around in another flick until he gets blown away all over again."

"Nothing seems real. Is that what you're saying?" Dani asked.

Austin's face turned serious as he continued. "We were in India for a year, and I saw a funeral procession go by every day. It was as common as a traffic jam is over here. You develop a different perspective on things like that when they're a regular part of your life. You don't freak out. It's just the way things are. People are born. People get sick. People die. Every minute of the day.

"In the good old US of A, people don't want to talk about these things. And when they have to, they don't know what to say, or how to act. No one ever thinks it can happen to him or to someone he cares about. And if it does—well, it's easier to try to ignore it or even act silly about it. To someone who is facing the terrible reality, it seems that people don't care—when they honestly don't know how to act."

His observations made sense, but Dani still found it hard to forgive Cassie's friends. "They could at least call her once in a while just to say, 'I don't know what to say.' That would be better than pretending she doesn't exist."

"I agree," he said. "But how are we going to change the world, Dani? Who's going to tell them how much it hurts?"

She didn't have an answer. She was hardly a crusader and wasn't sure anyone would listen to her even if she tried. She felt an overwhelming urge to cry. The tardy bell rang, and she opened the van door. As she hopped out, she said, "Thanks for the lift."

"Wait up. Would you like to do something after school?"

"I'm going right to the hospital."

"I could take you." He caught her arm. "Come on, Dani. I know it's bad for you, but don't run off."

Tears burned hot behind her eyes. She didn't want to have a crying fit in the school parking lot. She didn't want Austin to see her lose control. "I can catch the bus."

He kept hold of her arm and pulled her to him until she was captured against his broad, solid chest. It felt good to have somebody to lean on. She didn't pull away.

"Meet me here at three, and I'll drive you to the hospital," he told her. "You don't have to do this alone, Dani."

She nodded, not trusting her voice. He walked her into the building, his arm over her shoulder like a protective shield.

Seven

THAT AFTERNOON THEY arrived at the hospital and found Dani's mother looking frantic. "Mom! What happened?"

"Cassie had a convulsion. I'd just arrived. Nathan's in with her now." She buried her face in her hands.

Dani's knees felt rubbery. "Is she—is she—" Dani couldn't get the words out. Dr. Phillips emerged from Cassie's room, looking grim.

"I've put Cassie on an antiseizure medication. We'll put her in Intensive Care for the night for closer observation."

"I thought she was dying." Mom quietly cried,

and as Dr. Phillips took her hand to try to calm her, Dani realized her mother felt as helpless as she did.

Dani leaned against the wall, trying not to imagine Cassie thrashing uncontrollably on her bed.

"Could it happen again?" Dani heard her mother ask.

"Now that she's on the anticonvulsant, we think not."

"Has she suffered any permanent damage?"

"I don't know yet. I want to run another CAT scan and MRI."

Dani shivered. She knew how much Cassie disliked the scans. They weren't painful, but they were frightening. Cassie had explained that for the CAT scan, she had to lie perfectly still on a hard metal bed that moved slowly through a metal cylinder. She'd confided, "They put your head into some kind of bracelike contraption. The technicians are in another room, running the controls, so you're all alone with nothing but bright lights and the sounds of machinery. The room's ice-cold. It's all so impersonal, and you feel so vulnerable. I really hate it."

"Once she's stable, she'll come out of the ICU and back down to her room." Dr. Phillip's voice broke into Dani's thoughts. "Catherine, are you all right?"

"I'm frightened. From one day to the next, I don't know what to expect."

"Why don't you come up to the ICU while the nurses move Cassie," the doctor suggested.

Mom turned to Dani and Austin. "I think I'd better stay. Dani, why don't you go home."

"I'll take her home, Mrs. Vanoy. Don't worry."

Dani saw Cassie, who was heavily sedated and asleep, and then rode back to her house with Austin. "Would you like to come in?" she asked, realizing she wanted company.

"Sure. And if you've got a blender, I'll whip up one of my famous shakes."

"I don't want anything."

"You need to eat."

"Who are you, my mother?" She stalked away from the van and into the house.

He followed and caught up with her inside. He turned on some lights and made her sit on the sofa with him. "I wish there were something I could do for you," he said.

"There's nothing anyone can do. My sister's going to die, and all we can do is stand around and wait. Crazy, isn't it? You want to do something for me, and that's nice, but you can't. I want to do something for her."

"The two of you are pretty close, aren't you?"

"Cassie's always been there for me. We hardly ever fought when we were growing up. When I hear kids say how much they hate their sisters or brothers, I can't understand it. Things weren't perfect when we were younger, but we always got along. I remember once when I was eleven and got the flu, Cassie made me tomato soup and grilled cheese sandwiches. I'll never forget how good she was to me that day."

"You're lucky," Austin said. "I always wanted brothers and sisters, but I never got any. For my parents, work is their second child." He didn't sound bitter. "They feel their work is noble work—saving mankind—it's easy to get caught up in it, I guess. And in their life they've made time for me."

Dani realized that Austin had grown up to be a loner because he'd always spent so much time alone. He obviously wasn't antisocial. She liked that he was sensitive and kind. She appreciated him so much, but she didn't say anything. She didn't have much experience with boys. Her emotions were so mixed up that she didn't know what she was feeling for him. "The doctors were supposed to save Cassie, but they can't. All the things they know, and none of it can save my sister. My mother thinks Dr. Phillips is going to find some miracle. Fat chance."

Austin smiled ruefully. "That's why there's the other kind of saving, I guess. That's my missionary upbringing, of course. No one can be saved from dying, Dani."

She knew he was right, but that didn't make it any easier. "It just seems so unfair. Cassie had her whole life ahead of her."

"I know it doesn't make sense now, but one day it will. That's what faith is all about."

"You have faith, don't you, Austin?"

He nodded. "I know it isn't cool to admit such a thing, but it's true."

She envied him. All her life, she'd thought she had faith, but now, in the darkness of Cassie's dying, she felt lost and alone. Where was her faith now that she needed it?

Austin put his arm around her shoulder. She leaned against him, feeling weak. "Faith is a light that won't go out, Dani. It may get dim, it may even be hard to see because it's so dark, but it won't go out if you don't let it."

She sat with him in the soft yellow light of the living room, hoping to ignite the candle of her faith with his, while the sound of silence settled around them.

After Austin left, Dani climbed the stairs and prepared for bed. Her mother wasn't home yet. Dani went down the hall to Cassie's room and stood forlornly in the doorway. They had shared the room until Cassie had turned six and started school. She remembered the day her father had moved her into the third bedroom, which they'd used as a playroom up until that time. Dani had sobbed, not wanting to be separated from Cassie.

It was Cassie who had consoled her. "I'll read you a story every night." And for a long time, she did. At least until Dani could read by herself. But by then her father was dead and Mom worked full time and both girls had to go to day care every afternoon.

Dani entered the room and walked over to her sister's study desk. On top lay several college catalogues, including one for the University of South Florida in Tampa, where Cassie had marked the Marine Biology section. Dani's heart ached. She recalled the times Cassie had talked of college and of her dreams about working with sea life.

On Cassie's dresser were bows, barrettes and hair ribbons. Dani fingered them, realizing that Cassie would have no need of them now. She had no hair. Angrily, Dani yanked open the top drawer and shoved the offending hair paraphernalia inside. If only there was something she could do for her sister. Something grand and wonderful and memorable that would make her happy.

Sadly, Dani gazed about the room at her sister's belongings—her books, posters, photos, furniture. How empty the room looked without Cassie to bring it to life. Dani knew that Cassie's time was short, but Cassie didn't know it yet. She still had hopes and dreams. If only there was some way that Dani could snag one of Cassie's dreams and make it come true for her. If only . . .

Eight

❧

THE SEIZURE LEFT Cassie partially paralyzed on one side, and the newest scans and X rays showed that the radiation treatments had not slowed the growth of the tumor. Dani thought both pieces of news were cruel, but seeing Cassie struggling to speak, hold a fork, even walk, seemed more terrible.

Cassie grew despondent, and nothing anyone did cheered her up. Her gait looked peculiar because she dragged her left foot. She referred to herself as Igor, like the character in old horror movies. Dani knew that no matter how much headway Cassie made, it was simply a matter of time before the tumor's growth would win.

The following week, Austin took Dani to see Cassie at the hospital, but when they arrived at the door of her room, they heard the sounds of Cassie retching. Upset for her sister, Dani pushed Austin backward. "Maybe you'd better wait down the hall."

"Sure. Take as long as you want." He backed off, and she went into Cassie's room alone.

Two nurses were there. One held a basin, the other was helping Cassie lean forward. They spoke in encouraging voices, but Dani could hear little except Cassie's gagging and moaning. Each sound stabbed at her heart. When it was over, the nurses helped Cassie lie back. One offered Dani a sympathetic smile and said, "It's only a side effect. She had radiation today. She'll be all right as soon as she adjusts."

Only a side effect. Dani trembled, almost sick herself from the odors in the room and a sense of helplessness. The nurses left, and Dani stood over her sister, wondering if Cassie even knew she was there. Cassie's cheeks looked hollow, and her skin was gray. Pale blue veins shone through the thin skin of her eyelids. Dani watched as Cassie's parched lips tried to form words. She bent closer. "I'm right here, sis."

Cassie's lips moved, but still Dani could hear

no sound. She leaned far down, until her ear brushed Cassie's lips. "Tell me," Dani begged.

"No more," Cassie whispered. "Please. Tell them, no more."

Dani felt as if her heart might fragment into a million pieces. "I'll beat 'em off with a stick for you."

Cassie tried to smile, but the shape of her mouth crumpled and tears slid slowly from the corners of her eyes. "What did I do to deserve this? Was I an evil person? Did I offend God somehow and now I'm being punished?"

"You didn't do anything wrong," Dani insisted. "This just *happened* to you." She longed to say something encouraging to her sister, something profound and meaningful. All she could think of were cliches that sounded hollow.

Cassie turned her face toward Dani. "People say that suffering is supposed to make you a better person. That in the darkest times, a person has hope. I remember when Daddy died—how hopeless I felt. At first, I didn't think I could go on living without him."

"But you did. We all did." Dani remembered the horrible sense of loss she'd felt once she realized their father was never coming home again. "You have to hang on, Cassie. You have to keep going no matter how bad it hurts."

Cassie squeezed her eyes shut. "I'm trying," she

whispered. "There're so many things I want to do with my life. So much I want to see. I want to feel something besides pain and see something besides these hospital walls. There's a whole world right outside and I can't be a part of it. I want my life to count for something, Dani. I don't want to die before I get to do some of the things I've always wanted to do. Is that so wrong?"

Dani straightened, feeling as if she were being handed a sacred mission. Tears swam in her eyes, but they were overpowered by an unbelievable calm which began to build within her heart.

"I didn't mean to throw myself a pity party," Cassie said.

"You're entitled."

"No, I'm not. Pity parties are boring. Nobody wants to come to one."

Dani took Cassie's hand. "I'll come to whatever you want." She smoothed Cassie's cheek and came close to her sister's ear. Through the steely calm of her new found mission, she told her, "I'll help you out somehow. I promise."

That night, Dani formulated a plan. She turned the details over, examining every angle, then decided what to do. Carrying out her plan wasn't going to be easy. She would need Cassie's permission and she would need Austin's help in order to pull it off. She licked her lips nervously. Dani closed her eyes and prayed for the strength and courage to pull it off.

For the next two days, as Cassie recovered some of her strength, Dani plotted. When she was certain she had considered every detail, she cut out early from school and went to visit Cassie. Her sister was sitting up in bed, her face turned so that she could gaze out at the sunlight.

"Hi," Dani said.

"Hi, yourself." One side of Cassie's mouth drooped, so it was difficult for her to shape words.

"I want to ask you something." Dani came closer. She picked up Cassie's hand and held it. Since Cassie was able to keep food down, they'd removed her intravenous equipment, but Dani could see ugly bruises from the IVs.

"I've thought of some way to spend that money, if it's all right with you." Dani took a deep breath. "How would you like a trip to Florida? To the beach. To the same place your senior class went."

"That would be wonderful."

"I think we should use some of that One Last Wish money to take you there."

"You and me and Mom? No doctors?"

Dani plucked at the bed covers, searching for just the right words to explain. "Not Mom. At least, not at first."

"But we can't go without Mom."

"I'm telling you, Cassie, Mom won't allow it. She has a long list of reasons why we should stay here. So, I figure that you and I should just go, and once we get there, we'll call her and send her a ticket to fly down and stay with us." Dani spoke so rapidly that she was out of breath.

Cassie simply stared at her, wide-eyed. "Dani, that's crazy. But is it possible?"

She hadn't refused the idea. The realization propelled Dani to reveal more of her scheme. "We can do it! We won't stay long. We don't have to do anything you don't feel like doing. We can see the ocean and lie around the beach all day."

"How can we go to Florida without telling Mom?"

"We'll have to sneak away." Dani dropped her gaze because this was the truly tricky part of her plan.

"Sneak? But how?"

"We'll walk right out of the hospital together, late at night, between nurses' rounds. I've stayed here at night with you. I know how they schedule things, and I know we can do it."

Cassie frowned. "But then what? How will we get to Florida? You can't drive, and if we try to take a plane—well, I just think we'll get caught."

Dani thought so, too. Also, she wasn't sure she could handle buying plane tickets covertly. Anyway, even if she could, the airlines would have a record of where they went, and their mother would probably be waiting at the airport to catch them as soon as their plane touched the ground. And even though her plan was to call and tell Mom where they were once they got there, she didn't want to risk her goal of having Cassie see the ocean and walk the beach as she'd always dreamed of doing. "No. Flying's out," she told her sister. "Austin's driving us."

"Really?"

Dani took a deep breath. "Really. It's all arranged." She was lying, but knew that Cassie had to go along with the plan before she could beg Austin. "I told him we'll pay for everything—gas, food, whatever. All he has to do is get us there."

Cassie boosted herself up, awkwardly because she was still weak and uncoordinated on one side. For the first time in weeks, Dani saw color in her cheeks and brightness in her amber-brown eyes. "Can we really go? You're not just playing a trick on me?"

"Oh, sis, I'd never do anything so mean! I'm telling you, it's all worked out. All I need to do is cash the check for you, and we're out of here."

Cassie smiled like a conspiratorial child. "It'll have to be a secret, won't it?"

"The best-kept secret."

Cassie's expression clouded momentarily.

"What if I get sick while we're driving down there?"

Dani was pleased with herself, because she'd thought of that contingency, too. "Since it takes about a day and a half to drive, I figured we could leave between your radiation treatments, when you feel your best."

"What about my headaches?"

Dani knew how debilitating the attacks were, and as the tumor grew, Dr. Phillips warned, the headaches would get worse. "You have plenty of pain pills in the medicine cabinet at home. I'll bring them. And if things get unmanageable, we'll stop at the closest hospital. There are lots of big cities on the way to Florida. How hard can it be?"

"You're serious, aren't you?"

Cassie's question hardened Dani's resolve. "I know we can do it. It'll be a little tricky, but once we're on our way, it'll be a cinch."

"I don't feel right about Mom—"

"Look, I know she's going to be steamed, at first. But we'll leave her letters explaining that we had to go, and that we'll be fine, and that we'll call her once we get to where we're going. I think once she joins us and sees what a great time we can all have, she'll be okay about it. Mom's reasonable. She knows how much your senior trip meant to you."

Dani had rehearsed the speech so many times

that even she was beginning to believe it. "It's as if you're supposed to do this. While we don't know who gave you the money for a wish, I think you should use it to get something you've always wanted. Listen, even a trillion dollars can't make you well, but the money you've gotten *can* help you have some fun. I say let's go for it! You deserve to see the ocean, whether Mom agrees or not. I'm going to help you make your wish come true."

Nine

THE FRIDAY THAT school let out, Dani asked Austin to a movie. He picked her up that night, and although she sat through the entire feature, she didn't watch anything. Her mind was on other things. Afterward, she asked him to take her for a walk in a park that stretched along the Ohio River.

"So, what's on your mind?" he asked, startling her out of her contemplative mood.

"What makes you think I have something on my mind?" She tossed her mane of red hair.

"You've been a million miles away all night," he told her.

No use trying to stall, she told herself. She stopped walking and turned to face him. His face was in shadow, but his blond hair gleamed in the moonlight. Her heart thudded, and her palms began to perspire. "I'm going to take Cassie to Florida," she said softly. "To the beach."

"When did your mom change her mind about quitting the treatments?"

"She didn't."

"So, how . . . ?"

"I'm just taking her. That's all."

"Let me get this straight. You're going to take your dying sister on a trip that your mother doesn't know about and would never approve of?"

"That's right."

"Are you nuts?"

His tone stung her. For some reason, in her imagination, she'd pictured that Austin would nod his approval and ask, "How can I help?"

She glared at him. "No, I'm not nuts. I have it all planned out, and I know exactly what I'm doing."

"What exactly are you doing?"

"I'm taking Cassie for a vacation to see the ocean, because she doesn't have much time left. And because it's something I *have* to do." She eyed him defiantly. "I have money to pay for everything."

He was curious about her claim but only asked, "And what about your mother?"

"I'll call her when we get there, and she can come down and be with us. Once Cassie and I are down there, she'll have to come meet us."

"That's crazy."

"It's the only way I can get Cassie to Florida and do something for her."

He shook his head in disbelief and walked away, his hands shoved in his jean pockets. Over his shoulder, he asked, "And how are the two of you going to get down there—jump a freight train?"

"Don't make fun of me, Austin. I've thought of that, and I know *we* can do it."

He paused and turned slowly. His eyes were dark, but she could read his incredulous expression from ten feet. He asked, "We?"

She licked her lips and met the challenge of his gaze. "Right . . . we. I'm asking you to drive us. I need you, Austin. I need you to drive us in your parent's van. It's big enough so Cassie can lie down and be comfortable. It's new and dependable. The whole trip is only twenty hours. You can take us and leave us and come right back home."

He walked back over toward her. "Dani, there're three states between Ohio and Florida, and every major expressway will have cops alerted and on the lookout for you. No matter how good your intentions, you can't remove Cassie from the hospital without your mother's consent. You'll be breaking the law."

The police! Dani hadn't thought about maybe being chased by cops. With more determination than she felt, she said, "I don't care. We can make it . . . I know we can."

He turned away, but she grabbed his arm. "Please, Austin. You're the only one who understands how important this is. I thought you'd want to help Cassie. Even a stranger from the One Last Wish Foundation wants to help her, and so far as we know they've never met Cassie. If some strangers will reach out to her . . ." Dani let the sentence trail.

"What are you talking about—One Last Wish?"

Dani had decided she'd have to tell Austin. Now she told him about how Cassie had found the letter and the check. She didn't tell Austin the amount of the check. She thought that part was Cassie's to share. "I deposited the money in the bank."

"How did you do that? Didn't she have to sign or something?"

Dani nodded. "I took everything to Cassie at the hospital and after she signed the paperwork, I deposited the check," Dani said. "It's not hard to put money into the bank. It's hard to get it out. We have plenty of money to make the trip. After all, Cassie got the money and JWC told her to spend it on anything she wanted."

"I'm sure that didn't include kidnapping your sister and running away to Florida. Will there be enough left over for legal fees when the law catches up with you?"

Exasperated, Dani turned to pleading. "Austin, you once promised me you'd do anything you could to help Cassie. Did you lie?"

"Spiriting her out of the hospital and driving to Florida with every cop in the South looking for us, wasn't exactly what I had in mind in the way of helping."

Dani felt hot tears stinging her eyes. She couldn't start crying now! Furiously, she swiped the back of her hand over her eyes. Through gritted teeth, she fumed, "All right! So, don't help, Austin Cole. But don't think for a minute that just because you won't do it, I can't find somebody who will. I have enough money to rent a Learjet." She whirled on her heel and started walking back toward the car. "And forget about having to take me home. I'd rather walk!"

She hadn't gone far when he caught up to her and spun her around. She struggled to free herself, but felt all her inner reserves crumbling. Horrified, she began to weep.

"Don't cry," he whispered as he cradled her to him. "It'll be all right."

When she could talk, she sputtered, "It'll never be all right. Don't you see? Cassie's dying, and I can't stop it. No one can stop it. I've prayed and prayed for her to get well, but God's not answering. I don't even think He's listening."

"Don't be mad at God." Austin sighed. "You just have to believe that He knows what's going on with Cassie. And with you, too, you crazy girl. The bottom line is God gets to decide what happens, not us."

If she'd been playing a card game, Dani knew, she'd be out of aces. She'd tried everything, and still Austin had said no. For a few days, she had held some hope that she might be able to do something impossible and wonderful for her sister. Austin was right—she was nuts.

Dani let him hold her. She felt his fingers in her hair and listened to the beating of his heart through the fabric of his shirt. His voice sounded muffled as he said, "I don't want you finding someone else. I'll help you."

Her breath caught, and she hugged him tighter. "You will? You'll help me with my plan?"

He gazed down at her and, shaking his head, said, "It's a crazy idea that'll probably land us in jail, but your heart's in the right place, even if your brain isn't." He paused and touched her cheek. "Besides, if Cassie were my sister, I'd want to do the same thing for her."

"You're really going to help," she said, as if the words were a magic chant. Suddenly, she felt as though a weight had been removed from her shoulders. "I'm so sorry I yelled at you. You're wonderful, honest!"

"I'm not doing this just for Cassie," he said. "I'm doing it for you, too."

"Because we're friends?"

"Because we're friends and because, Dani, you're somebody special to me."

Dani sprang into activity over the next few days to get things ready from the van to finding a hotel. She and Austin pored over road maps, choosing the best routes. If they couldn't take I-75 and the other major highways, they'd turn off the beaten path. Dani had no intentions of being stopped by the police and sent home before they reached their destination.

The plan was in place on Monday morning once her mother went to work. Dani packed suitcases. She carefully chose a selection of summer and beach clothes she'd bought at the mall. Austin organized the van. He filled a cooler with drinks, snacks, and bags of food they'd bought at the supermarket. The less they had to stop, the better off they would be, they'd decided.

Austin arranged a pallet and thick mat on the carpeted floor of the van for Cassie. They lined it with blankets and pillows, leaving room for Dani to be near Cassie if necessary. Austin rigged a battery-powered small reading lamp and selected books and magazines. The van was air-conditioned and that would help them not have to deal with the heat.

Austin piled other boxes under the seats and explained to Dani that he'd organized "support equipment," in case they came up against anything unexpected.

Cassie's treatment on Monday made her sick. Dani held her hand and assured her that things were almost ready. "I'm supposed to get another radiation treatment on Thursday," Cassie said. "I can't stand it anymore. I'd be better off dead."

Dani's stomach tightened with both dread and anticipation. "We'll leave Wednesday night," she promised her sister. "Right after the midnight shift change. The nurses won't check vital signs until about three A.M. That'll give us a good head start."

"I can hardly wait," Cassie whispered. "So much has happened. This really is going to be my wish come true."

Dani tried to take a nap Wednesday, but she was too tense to sleep. As she and her mom headed home from their visit to Cassie, her mother said, "You know, I think in spite of everything, the radiation's helping."

"How so?" Dani asked nervously.

"Didn't you see how happy Cassie looked to-night? How bright her eyes were? How talkative she was? I'm telling you, Dani, she was almost glowing. I know she's responding to the treatments."

"Dr. Phillips told us she'd have good times along with the bad."

"You see, I was right to insist on the treatments," Mom said with a grin. "Cassie may lick this thing after all."

"Maybe," Dani agreed, feeling like a traitor. In a few hours, she, Cassie, and Austin would be on the road to Florida. There would be no turning back. She tried not to listen to her mother's chatter. She concentrated on making her sister's wish come true.

Ten

WEDNESDAY NIGHT, WHILE her mother was sound asleep, Dani noiselessly stole down the stairs. Outside, the moonless night seemed very dark. Austin had pulled the van to the end of her street, and she climbed inside. Wordlessly, Austin drove to the hospital and parked as close to an emergency side exit as possible. Austin waited in the van while Dani walked boldly through the Emergency Room entrance.

The ER waiting area was crowded, and no one even noticed her. She rode up to Cassie's floor and slipped off the elevator. The corridor lights had been dimmed, and the halls were deserted.

The ever present hospital smell hung in the air. Only the sounds of respirators and the beep of heart monitors seemed threatening.

Dani held her breath. She purposely bypassed Cassie's room, opened the inner stairwell door, and hurried down seven flights of stairs. At the fire door leading outside, she paused to catch her breath and slow her pounding heart. As quietly as she could, she opened the door, always locked at night from the outside, and let Austin in. He brushed past her, and together, they headed back up.

She prayed every step of the way that no nurse or technician would choose this time to take the stairs. On Cassie's floor, Dani cracked the heavy fire door and peered both ways. "All clear," she whispered over her shoulder.

Cautiously, she and Austin slipped inside and went straight to Cassie's room. Her sister was waiting for them. Dani had left clothes for her sister, and Cassie had found the strength to get dressed. She'd tied a scarf around her hair which was still patchy from the treatments. As Austin helped Cassie out of bed, Dani arranged the pillows and some towels from the bathroom so that from the doorway, it looked as if someone were still in the bed.

At the doorway of the room, Dani held her breath and peeked out. Again, the long, quiet corridor was unoccupied. *Two minutes*, she told herself. That's all the time they needed to get to the fire door. She went first, opened the door, and slid around the corner. Keeping it partially open, she gave Austin a hand signal, and he scooped Cassie up in his arms and hurried for the opening.

Dani shut the door, and the three of them stood in the stairwell for a moment.

"We're all sure we want to do this?" Dani asked suddenly.

"Let's go," Cassie said.

Austin half carried Cassie, half supported her down the stairs with Dani leading the way. At the bottom, Dani darted outside and opened the door of the van. She got in and watched as Austin carried Cassie across the short space from the doorway to where the van was parked.

Dani helped Cassie inside, settling her onto the mat. Austin hopped behind the steering wheel and turned on the motor. Kneeling beside her sister, Dani asked, "You okay?"

Cassie's breath was coming in short, gasping bursts. "I'm okay," she whispered. "We made it."

Dani grasped her sister's hand, resting it alongside her perspiring cheek. "Let's hope so," she told her as the van began to move.

Cassie quickly fell asleep, obviously exhausted just from the escape. Dani sat in the front of the van on the passenger's side. "She doing all right?" Austin asked.

"It took a lot out of her, but she's coasting on adrenaline. I haven't seen her this excited since last Christmas—before she got sick." Dani grinned. She felt afraid but satisfied.

Austin glanced in his side mirror and accelerated up the ramp marked "I-75 South." Leaving Cincinnati, so near to the border between Ohio and Kentucky, they were into the Bluegrass State in no time. Since the expressway was practically deserted, Dani didn't feel the need to keep looking over her shoulder for police lights.

Austin flipped on the cruise control mechanism and settled back in the seat with a long sigh. "Don't want to break any speed limits."

"We made it," Dani said, keeping her eyes straight ahead. She experienced a wave of euphoria.

"So far."

"Getting her out of the hospital was the hardest part," she countered.

"Don't bet on it."

"What do you mean?"

"I figure that if we're lucky, they won't discover she's missing for another two hours. Then they'll call your mother. Then she'll call the police—"

"We left letters for her, explaining everything," Dani interrupted.

He shook off her remark and continued. "The police will start pumping your mother for information on who could have helped you. And before too long, your mom will think of me. Then the police will come and find out that I told my neighbor I was going off for a few days—"

"You told your neighbor?" Dani scowled at him.

"Someone had to take care of my dog." He ignored her angry look. "And once the cops and your mom figure out I'm driving, they'll issue an all-points bulletin for my arrest—"

"All right! All right! Why didn't you mention the dog before? What's your point now? Are you thinking of turning around and going back? Because if you are—"

"I'm not. I'm just doing a mental outline of a possible scenario. We need to be prepared."

"We *are* prepared."

"My guess is that we've got about six hours of driving time left on this road."

"We discussed this already."

"We'll have to hit some of those rural back roads we marked on the map."

"It'll be daylight in six hours," she observed nervously, feeling safer under the cover of night.

"That's right. And by seven, with any luck, we should be through the Cumberland Gap and crossing into Tennessee."

Dani's palms were sweating. "That'll be good. One state behind us by morning."

"You don't understand," he said. "We *have* to be through the Cumberland Gap by then, because this is about the only road through those mountains."

"How bad can it be?"

He snorted and said, "It's no fun, especially in fog."

Dani stared blankly out of the windshield, trying not to think about the anguish her mother would be facing when she first heard that Cassie and she were missing. The soft sounds of the radio, the dimness of the interior made her feel protected. Soon, her eyelids grew heavy and she couldn't hold them open.

Austin reached behind his seat and fished out a pillow. He handed it over, and she settled into it gratefully. She didn't know how long she slept when she startled upright. "What's wrong?"

"Fog," he said grimly. "It'll really slow us down."

Outside, the world had lightened to a pale gray, but the van was shrouded in a thick cloud of mist. "I can't see anything."

"If you could, you'd see that we're going up a mountain with sheer rock on one side and a guard rail on the other between us and a thousand foot dropoff."

"You must be tired, too. Can we stop?"

"And have some trucker plow into us?" He had already turned on his lights and now set his flasher signal. "Maybe this will help someone see us so we don't get rear-ended."

She understood what he meant when minutes later, the massive back end of a creeping semi loomed in front of them without warning. Dani gasped.

Austin braked. "Imagine doing this by wagon train like Daniel Boone."

"It's a wonder anyone ever went west," she complained. One thing about their part of Ohio—it was flat. And so was the road to Iowa. Flat, dark soil dressed up with standing fields of corn and grain.

"How's Cassie?" Austin wanted to know.

Dani unbuckled her seat belt and moved to the back of the vehicle. "Still sleeping." In the gray light of morning, her sister looked so fragile and pale that the enormity of what they were doing struck Dani hard. A very sick girl was miles away from medical help, inside a van that was crawling like a snail up the foggy side of a mountain. Dani swallowed down a sick feeling that rose in her throat.

"We'll make it," Austin called. "The fog's lifting."

Through the windshield, Dani saw the fog part

in wispy sprays, like angel hair. Beyond lay the sprawling mountain splendor of the great Cumberlands. Wide-eyed, she gazed down at valleys, thick with trees, green with the ripening of summer. Rays from a rising morning sun were glorious. She didn't speak all the way down the road through the Gap, awed by the beauty, overwhelmed by the splendor.

Less than an hour later, their van crossed into Tennessee.

Eleven

THEY PULLED INTO a gas station at the next exit, Austin filled the van's gas tank, and they got back on the road. Cassie awoke, hungry. While Austin drove, Dani handed Cassie a muffin, "It shouldn't make you nauseous," Dani said.

"What would you like?" she asked Austin.

"Make me a sandwich. It'll be easy to eat while I drive."

Dani prepared the sandwich, then sat in the back on the floor with her sister and ate a muffin, too. Cassie reached for her duffel bag. "Did you pack my conch shell?"

Dani helped her root through the bag until she

found the large pink shell. Cassie held it to her ear and smiled. "I can hardly believe I'll be seeing the ocean soon." Then, a frown crossed her face. "Mom probably knows by now that we're gone."

"It's a good bet."

"She's going to be awfully upset and angry."

"I know."

"Dani, I told her that in my letter that it was all *my* idea. That I begged you to take me. I told her about the One Last Wish money and how you were going to help me make my wish come true. I told her we were only using a little of the money. The rest is for the bills and everything. I hope she forgives me."

"I told her that it was all *my* idea. I wanted you to have a fabulous weekend. I wrote that we'd call her as soon as we got to where we wanted to go."

"She'll figure out that we're headed to the beach."

"Probably so, but there are an awful lot of beaches in the world."

Cassie held up her hand to put an end to the conversation. She glanced toward the driver's seat. "So, tell me, Austin. How did my sister ever talk you into this crazy idea?"

"I figured a trip to Florida would be the perfect way to kick off an otherwise boring summer. Anyway, I've been all over the world, but never to Florida with two babes!"

"I think it's nice of you," Cassie said. "And real nice of your parents to let us use their van."

Dani held her breath, hoping that Cassie wouldn't ask any more questions. It wouldn't take much for Cassie to figure out Dani had not told her the truth. Dani hadn't wanted to worry her, so she'd purposely been vague about the details and the dangers. Inwardly, all Dani hoped for was that things would go smoothly and they would reach their destination without trouble.

She and Cassie played a game of cards, but by midmorning, Cassie started complaining of a headache. Dani's stomach knotted. She gave her sister a painkiller, the same she received in the hospital. But the pain didn't subside. Soon, Cassie was drenched with sweat and sick to her stomach. "I need to stop," she mumbled.

"We have to stop, Austin," Dani said urgently.

He got off the expressway at the next exit and pulled into a McDonald's lot. Dani helped Cassie into the bathroom, where Cassie vomited violently. Dani stood beside her as she retched over the toilet. "The pain . . ." Cassie mumbled. "It's never been this bad."

Dani was so afraid, she felt numb all over. "Maybe you can take another pill?"

"I can't keep it down." Cassie gagged.

"But if you were back in the hospital—"

"They'd give me a shot."

Dani felt panic. She had no shots for Cassie. She dampened a wad of paper towels, which she applied to the back of Cassie's neck. "We need to get out of here," she told Cassie gently. "Can you make it now? Try to take another pill."

"I'll try."

Dani helped Cassie to her feet and outside to the van. Austin was studying a map. "She doesn't look much better," he whispered to Dani.

The two of them helped Cassie to lie down as Dani explained that Cassie couldn't keep her medication down. "Give me the bottle," he said.

He removed one of the pills, crushed it in a cup, added water, and made a paste. "Smear this on her gums and on the inside of her mouth," he directed.

With trembling hands, Dani obeyed.

"She'll absorb the medication through her gums, and it'll bypass her stomach."

Dani believed him because she had no choice. Once she was finished, Austin began to drive south along a back road that paralleled I-75. Dani held Cassie's hand and chewed her bottom lip while Cassie moaned, but within twenty minutes, her groaning began to lessen, and she fell asleep.

"It worked," Dani said, climbing into the passenger seat.

"Good." Austin tossed her the map. "We're going to have to stop for the day."

"But we're barely past Knoxville."

"No choice. She needs to rest during the heat of the day, and I could stand a little sleep myself."

Austin had been driving nonstop since midnight. Of course, he was exhausted. "Where should we stop?"

"One of these dirt side roads." He found one he liked and took it. Then he pulled off and drove the van carefully through the woods under the cover of trees. When he came to a clearing, he shut off the engine.

Dani was struck by the silence of the summer forest. Bright sunlight flowed through the leafy canopy, and the air grew still and hot. "Come on," Austin said, getting out of the van. "Help me set up camp."

"Camp?"

"Don't tell me you've never camped before?"

"Sure—under my mother's dining room table with a blanket thrown over the top."

He laughed. "Well, it's time you learned how to rough it." He opened up the side of the van, and without disturbing Cassie, he hauled out a large bundle.

"What's that?"

"A tent. Give me a hand."

She followed his instructions, and soon they had a canvas roof and floor attached to the open side of the van. A thin, screenlike netting, to keep out insects, made up the sides of the enclosure. They spread out bedrolls and turned on portable fans to circulate the air. With Cassie sound asleep in the van, Austin stretched out on the canvas-covered ground. "You should get some sleep, too," he told Dani with a yawn.

She lay down, but said, "I'm not going to be able to sleep."

"You'd better—we've got a whole night of driving ahead of us."

She turned on her side and stared out at the woods through the fine mesh screen. The world looked lazy and peaceful, but Dani was still feeling the strain of their ordeal. Half under her breath, she said, "I was so scared back in that bathroom, Austin."

Austin moved closer to her. "She was pretty sick?"

Dani nodded. "She couldn't stop throwing up. It really hit me that we're out here with no doctors and only a limited amount of medicine."

"We can turn back."

She shook her head. "That would be even worse." Dani rolled over so that she was staring into Austin's eyes. "What if . . . what if . . . Cassie dies? Mom would never forgive me. I'd never forgive myself."

"I thought you told me you have everything figured out."

"I do," she insisted fiercely. "But when I saw Cassie so sick . . . I felt so helpless . . . I don't know. I'm scared."

"You've got more than one good reason," he said.

"What do you mean, Austin? Has something happened you haven't told me about? Can you still drive?"

He sighed. "You'd better know. While you were in the bathroom at the McDonald's, I turned on the radio and heard the news." He took a deep breath. "The police are looking for us."

Twelve

❧

Dani imagined hundreds of law enforcement agents combing the countryside looking for them. "I thought we'd have more time. What exactly was said?"

"The report said that anyone who saw a black van with Ohio license plates should notify the police."

"I'm sorry," she whispered, squeezing her eyes shut. "I didn't want to turn us into criminals."

"Hey," he said, smiling at her stricken face. "I'm a big boy. I knew what I was getting into."

His expression looked reassuring, and for a moment Dani felt less guilty. "You're not mad at me?"

"No." He lay back down, his hands clasped behind his head, and stared up at the top of the tent. "But I think we'd better not play the radio while we travel. Cassie doesn't need to hear that we're being sought as runaways."

"You're right. No need to upset her," Dani agreed.

"We just have to hang on," he said. "And we'll have to be very careful. We'll drive at night and sleep by day. I brought a Coleman stove, so before we take off tonight, we'll cook some supper and eat it here. I don't want to take the chance of going into a restaurant."

"I'll bet someone from the McDonald's will remember us."

"It's a possibility, but there's nothing we can do about it."

Dani tried to close her eyes, but her dream of taking Cassie to the beach seemed to be turning into a nightmare. What if Cassie got sick—so sick that she . . . Dani broke out in a cold sweat and forced her thoughts in a different direction. She glanced at Austin, resting beside her and felt an overwhelming sense of gratitude toward him. No one else could have helped her pull this off. "How did you learn all this camping stuff, Austin?"

He raised up on one elbow. "What stuff?" She gestured at her surroundings. "When we lived in

Africa, we'd take trips to villages with no modern conveniences. All the missionaries have simple medical and first aid training. Out in the bush, you never know what you'll run into."

"What was it like living in Africa?"

"In many ways, it was beautiful. The land was wild and untamed. We took barges down the Congo and drove Land Rovers through the plains. There were no paved roads in the back country, and hardly even any dirt ones. Driving over some of the territory, it felt as if your teeth were vibrating out of your head."

"Were there wild animals?"

"Sure. At night, you could hear the hyenas howling, but we had guides and bearers, natives who helped carry the gear. We learned a lot from the natives, as much as we taught them! They always lit fires around the perimeters of our camp when the sun went down. No Holiday Inns or hotels along the way. We camped under the stars."

"And you were in India, too?"

"For a year. But I liked Africa best. Too many people in India."

Dani turned to face him. "Did you spend a lot of time alone or with your parents?"

"There were schools in the big cities, and that's where we were based most of our time. My mom and dad are teachers. I went to classes with rich locals and other MKs—missionary kids. In the summers, we traveled."

"Cassie always wanted to travel," Dani said wistfully.

"I'm glad she only wanted to go to Florida this trip, and not Tahiti."

His joke made her smile. "Do you miss life abroad?"

"Sometimes. Not just the land, but the seriousness of everyday life. Whenever I'd come back to the States with my folks to raise money to help support their mission work, I couldn't believe how spoiled American kids are. I mean, they spend half a day watching TV and the rest of the day saying they're bored. If people didn't work every day in India or Africa, they'd die."

"How did you spend your time in those places?"

"I helped with chores—farming, digging wells, taking care of livestock. But I had fun, too. All missionary families lived together in a compound. We played soccer a lot. We kicked oranges when we didn't have a ball."

Dani gazed intently at him. What a strange and different kind of life he'd led. "I guess it hasn't been easy fitting in over here."

"No joke." His laugh held no humor. "When kids find out you're an MK, they treat you as if you're some kind of alien. As if you might burst into Bible verses. They don't realize that you're interested in the same things as every other kid your age."

"Is that why you wear your hair long?"

"Maybe. I'd get an earring, but Dad would croak."

"Are your parents thinking of leaving Cincinnati?"

"Would you miss me?" He flashed a grin at her.

"Not a bit," she said, knowing it wasn't true. She peeked up at him shyly. "Okay . . . maybe just a little. Who'd take me camping and help me make my sister's dream come true?"

He stared at her in such a way, she turned her head. No boy had ever looked at her that way before. She swallowed hard, unable to sort out what she was experiencing.

With a sudden laugh, Austin tousled her hair and flopped back down. He rolled over and said, "Go to sleep. It'll be nighttime before you know it."

Dani puzzled over the sensations pouring through her. Austin was helping her accomplish one of her most important missions in life, and she felt grateful to him. What else could it be? This trip was for Cassie, not for herself. She'd better not forget what it was all about.

Dani awoke with a start. Beside her, Austin slept, looking as peaceful as a small child. She inched away and crept inside the van. Cassie was sitting with her legs crossed. The lamp was on, and she was staring at a magazine.

"Hey," Dani said. "You feeling better?"

Cassie shrugged. "A little dopey. I think it's the medicine."

"Good magazine?"

Cassie shook her head. "I can't read it, really. The type looks blurry, and sometimes I see double pages."

Dani didn't like the sound of her sister's description.

"The medicine's never done this before."

"Well, I never had to glue it in your mouth before."

Cassie snickered, and Dani felt relieved knowing her sister's sense of humor was intact. "I guess it was pretty weird," Cassie said. "I'll bet we scared off half of those McDonald's customers forever."

"I hear Ronald McDonald himself is out to get us."

Cassie laughed aloud.

"Did I miss a good joke?" Austin stepped inside the van, his eyes still heavy with sleep.

"We didn't mean to wake you," Dani apologized.

"No problem. We've got to start packing up,

anyway." He looked at his watch. "I'd like to be rolling in an hour."

"I'm hungry," Cassie said.

Dani flipped open the ice chest, glad to think about something as ordinary as eating. "Soup— coming up."

"Gosh, I hope not!" Cassie replied in wide-eyed innocence. "I'm tired of having my food come up."

The three of them looked at each other, then burst into laughter. Quickly, they set about fixing dinner as twilight fell over the Tennessee woods. An hour later, they pulled out onto the highway, heading south.

Thirteen

⁓

"WHY DON'T WE put on some music?" Cassie suggested.

"Cassette of your choice," Austin said. He popped open the glove compartment, and Dani rummaged for a tape—any tape—knowing it was important to keep the radio off.

When the music was playing, Cassie sat forward on a stack of pillows, directly behind the console and between the two front seats. "Where are we?" she asked.

"About an hour from Atlanta. From there, it's around five hours to the Florida state line."

"And to the beach?"

"Another four hours to Melbourne."

Dani made a quick mental calculation and figured they'd be hitting their destination around five A.M. She felt a stirring of excitement—they might make it after all, despite all the setbacks.

"I can't wait," Cassie said eagerly. "Where are we going to stay?"

"All arranged," Dani announced. "I reserved rooms at a beachfront hotel—as we know, money is no object. Thanks to our wonderful, mysterious One Last Wish friend I reserved us two rooms."

"You didn't choose the same hotel my class stayed at?"

"Of course not."

"Did you use your name to make the reservations?" Austin asked quickly.

"I have more sense than that. I used Smith."

"Smith?" Austin and Cassie asked in unison.

"What's wrong with Smith?"

"You could have been more original," Austin teased. "Don't you think so, Cassie?"

"Dani, anyone could have thought of something better than Smith."

Dani glanced from one to the other. "Well, excuse me. The next time I plan a getaway weekend to Florida, I'll be sure and consult with you two over an appropriate name for registration."

"Touchy, isn't she?" Austin asked Cassie.

"I don't know what I'm going to do with her,"

Cassie said with an exaggerated sigh. "Kidnapping patients from hospitals, dragging people into the woods to camp by *day*, and choosing a name like Smith . . . She's such an ordinary kind of sister."

"That's for sure," Austin agreed.

Dani ignored him. "And what name would you have picked, Miss Originality?"

Cassie contemplated for a moment. "How about something exotic, like Madame Bovary, or mysterious, like Mr. Heathcliff."

"Or something famous, like Washington," Austin interjected.

"I still prefer Smith," Dani insisted. "It's the perfect name if you two think about it. And if you give me any more grief, I'll call ahead and cancel the rooms." She tried to keep a straight face to accompany her threat.

"Smith sounds okay to me," Cassie said quickly.

"Works for me," Austin said.

Dani gave them both a smug grin. "And you didn't think I could be flexible."

About one A.M., as they crossed the Florida state line, they cheered. Looking at the gas gauge, Austin said, "We'd better stop and fill up." He pulled into a service station, where the neon brightness made Dani squint.

She and Cassie went to the ladies' room while

Austin pumped gas. Dani couldn't help noticing how slowly Cassie moved. She was dragging her left foot more than usual.

"I'm just stiff," Cassie explained apologetically. "From sitting so long."

"I know what you mean," Dani assured her. "So am I."

Cassie glanced up and around. "You'd think they'd light these places better at night."

"Are you serious? It's bright as—" She checked herself and asked, "What do you mean?"

"Everything looks sort of dim. Don't you think so?"

Was something happening to Cassie's eyesight? Dani wondered. "I can see well enough to get us to the bathroom and back," Dani said.

"Good. I wouldn't want to trip."

In the bathroom, Dani splashed cold water on her face, hoping to settle the sick feeling in the pit of her stomach. She recalled Dr. Phillips's warning that as the tumor grew, so would Cassie's physical symptoms. Her sister had to be all right. In less than a day, they'd be at the beach.

Dani opened the bathroom door and stepped outside. She stopped in her tracks as she noticed the Florida highway patrol car parked by the gas pumps. Fear squeezed her pounding heart. By reflex, she stepped back inside the bathroom.

"What's wrong?" Cassie asked.

"Uh . . . Austin's not ready yet."

"So, can't we go sit in the van and wait for him?"

Dani scrambled for a reasonable excuse, but came up empty. Haltingly, she said, "Look . . . Cassie . . . there's a cop outside . . . and I think . . . it would be best . . . if we waited until he left."

Cassie stared at her, one eyelid and one side of her mouth drooping noticeably. "Are the police searching for us?"

"It's possible." Dani tried to sound unconcerned.

"I want to go to the beach," Cassie said. Tears shimmered in her eyes, making Dani's heart ache.

"We'll go," she assured her. "But I think we should wait until the cop leaves—just to be safe."

Cassie leaned against the wall, covered her face with her hands, and slid to the floor. Dani didn't know how to console her.

"I don't want to g-go h-home," Cassie repeated, sobbing.

"It'll be all right," Dani said gently. "Let me take a peek outside."

She cracked the door, but could still see the patrol car. Why didn't it go away? She saw Austin, too. He was leisurely washing the van's windshield. She also saw that he'd put on a baseball cap and tucked his long, blond ponytail under it. She admired his ingenuity.

Dani continued to watch through the opening. She couldn't see the patrolman, and assumed he was inside the convenience store of the gas station. She saw Austin complete his window-cleaning chore, then climb inside the van. She heard him start the engine and for a moment felt confused. What did he want her and Cassie to do? Run and jump in the van? Surely, that would cause an uproar. And he knew that Cassie couldn't run.

As she continued to watch, unsure of what to do, the van started moving. Dani saw it make a slow, wide arc and turn back in the opposite direction, pull out onto the road, and head off. She blinked, incredulous and uncomprehending as its taillights disappeared in the darkness.

She clutched the door handle until her hand hurt, but she didn't move. From the floor beside her, she heard Cassie's soft sobs. Dani felt trapped. She took deep breaths, trying to calm her nerves and get a grip on her emotions. Austin couldn't leave them stranded. He just couldn't!

Moments later, Dani saw the highway patrolman come out to his car, get inside, and start off. She had to open the door wider and crane her neck to see him driving away, because he was headed in the other direction from the van, but once he was out of sight, she opened the door completely and urged Cassie to her feet. The bathroom had grown hot and stuffy, and sweat was pouring off her face.

"It'll be cooler outside," she told her sister, who followed like a docile child.

"Did the policeman go away?" Cassie asked.

"Yes." *And so did Austin*, Dani thought.

Suddenly, the van appeared in front of them. Austin leapt out and hurried up to them. "Are you two all right?" His face was as white as a sheet.

Dani was so relieved to see him that she almost hugged him. "We're fine, and the cop's gone."

"I saw him leave. I pulled off to the side of the road up ahead"—he nodded in the direction he'd come from—"and turned off my lights and waited until he left." Austin helped Cassie inside, and once he and Dani were in with the doors locked, he backed the van out and continued on their original route.

Cassie curled up on the floor with a blanket and fell asleep. Neither Dani nor Austin said a word for several miles. Dani folded her hands in her lap to conceal their trembling. She felt drained and shaky. Staring straight ahead, she mumbled, "When I heard your engine start, I didn't know what to do."

"It was the only thing I could think to do." Austin sounded subdued. "I didn't want to make him suspicious. I kept praying that you'd stay inside the bathroom. That you'd trust me enough to wait for me."

Dani looked at him. "At first, I thought you'd left us."

He glanced at her sharply, a look of hurt on his face. "Don't you know, Dani? I'm in this all the way with you. I won't leave you. Not even when it's all over."

She kept silent. When it was over, she might need him more than ever.

Fourteen

~~~

Dᴀɴɪ sᴀᴛ ǫᴜɪᴇᴛʟʏ as miles and miles of highway slid past the window of the van. Dawn began to break in cool gray strips, and stars blinked out, as if some hand were turning them off, one by one. Her eyes felt gritty, and there was a stale, unpleasant taste in her mouth, left over from doughnuts and colas at three ᴀ.ᴍ.

Austin had taken a chance on a more direct route. He'd picked up the Florida Turnpike, then a state road going east. Every muscle in Dani's body ached, and all she wanted to do was stretch out in a soft, clean bed and sleep. She thought of home and her bedroom. She'd been gone two nights, but it seemed so much longer.

"Once we get through town, we'll pick up the beachfront highway and go to the hotel," Austin said, breaking the monotonous droning sound of the engine and tires that filled the van.

"We can't check in till noon," Dani replied with a tired sigh.

"Then we'll just wait on the beach. I'm guessing that people will start showing up early, so we won't be noticed among the crowds." He glanced back at Cassie. "She sleeps a lot."

"It's part of her symptoms. But it's better that she does. It's making the trip shorter for her."

The day continued to brighten, and Cassie stirred. She sat up and gazed out the window. "Are we at the beach yet?"

"Almost," Austin answered cheerfully. "Do you want to stop for a minute?"

"No. Please, let's go to the water." There was a sense of urgency in her voice.

Austin continued to drive until he found a deserted parking lot designated for public beach access. He rolled to a stop. The moment the doors opened, Dani caught the sharp, tangy scent of the sea air and heard the muffled rhythmic beat of water hitting the shore. A morning breeze blew soft and balmy, stirring her hair and reviving her spirits.

They walked along a short wooden boardwalk, over a crest of sand, and saw the sea stretching calmly before them. "May I present the Atlantic Ocean," Austin said with a flourish.

Dani watched Cassie. She wondered if her sister felt the way she did—overwhelmed, almost giddy. No movie, no TV image, no photograph had been equal to what lay in front of them. The shoreline stretched endlessly in either direction, and in the distance, the sky appeared to meet the water at the horizon. The sight left her speechless.

Cassie's eyes were bright and she was smiling. She slipped off her shoes and touched her toes to the sand. "I want to feel the water." She started to walk across the thick, heavy sand with her lurching gait.

Dani followed, then Austin. At the edge of the water, Cassie stopped, took a deep, long breath, flung her arms wide open, and raised her face to the brightening sky. "I made it! My wish has been granted." She reached over to hug Dani and then Austin. "This is a view I could never have from my hospital bed!" And she laughed.

They walked along the shore and saw the sunrise. Rays glistened on the water like jewels. Dani's eyes darted everywhere. As she stood still, the water sucked the sand away from her feet, leaving indentations that slowly vanished as every passing wave swept over it.

When Cassie grew tired of walking, they sat in the sand and gazed out at a sea that had changed from gray to green with the rising of the sun. The sky turned blue, and small, puffy white clouds appeared. Dani sifted white sand through her fingers.

"It's more beautiful than I ever imagined," Cassie said. "Coming here was worth it all. I hope Mom understands."

The sun was growing warmer, and Dani felt its heat on her head and back.

"I think we should go have a healthy breakfast and then check in to our rooms," Austin said.

Dani's stomach growled at the suggestion, causing the three of them to laugh.

"We can come back to the beach, can't we?" Cassie asked, her expression eager.

"That's why we're here, isn't it?" Austin helped her to her feet, and they all walked back to the van.

At the restaurant, Dani and Austin ordered big meals. Cassie said she wasn't very hungry.

Dani ate ravenously when the food arrived. Austin bought a newspaper and flipped through it, handing it over to Dani, and pointing discreetly to a small story on an inside page. The headline read: "Teens Flee Hospital." She stopped eating and read the story. According to the account, a teenage boy and girl from Ohio had taken the girl's sister, who was a cancer patient, from a Cincinnati hospital. No trace of them had been found thus far, but police were searching. A reward was offered. Dani was grateful that their names weren't printed.

Dani continued to skim the paper. "Cassie," she said, "this article says that a bunch of loggerhead turtles will be released from one of the beaches around here. Didn't we just see a TV show about that?"

Cassie brightened. "Yes. I remember. I'd really like to see that."

"A turtle release?" Austin commented, as if both of them had lost their wits. "Sounds like a yawn to me."

Cassie became more animated as she explained, "Austin, this is an endangered species. The mother turtles crawl up on the beach and lay their eggs and cover them, then about two months later, the baby turtles hatch and head toward the sea. But between the development of the beachfront and natural enemies, not many of the little turtles make it. Sometimes, rangers dig up the eggs, and as the eggs start to hatch, they bring them back to the beach and release them. That way, the turtles have a better chance of surviving."

Austin still didn't look impressed.

"If I could," Cassie continued, "I'd be a marine biologist and help protect all the animals facing extinction in the ocean. Wouldn't it be a terrible world without whales, or dolphins, or turtles?"

"Yes, it would. But I think we should go check in to our rooms now, and talk about sea creatures later," Dani said with a tired yawn.

Austin agreed. Dani picked up the check, and they went to find their hotel.

Their rooms adjoined on the ground floor and faced the ocean. Sliding glass doors opened out onto a small patio set in the sand. Austin took one room and helped the girls unload their suitcases in the other.

Dani took a long, hot shower, but Cassie couldn't be persuaded to do anything except sit on the patio lounge chair and gaze out at the sea.

"Austin's in his room, but he said to let him know if we want to do anything," Cassie said when Dani emerged from the steamy bathroom.

"We should call Mom," Dani announced. "It's time."

Cassie gazed at the horizon. "Not yet."

"Why? You know she's worried." Now that they were actually at the beach, Dani felt really guilty about running away.

"Later."

"But—"

"Please." Cassie glanced skyward. "It's getting cloudy. Maybe it's going to rain. Let's go shopping. I've been in the hospital for weeks. I'd love to just poke around some stores. I haven't been shopping in ages. We could buy something nice for Mom. A peace offering. We have enough money to get her something nice."

Dani eyed her carefully. Cassie's eyes were bright, but she looked frail. "You sure you're strong enough?"

"If I get tired, we can come right back." Cassie added, "You don't think Austin will mind, do you? I guess he must be tired. You must be tired, too. Maybe he's asleep."

"Let me get dressed and go tell Austin," Dani said. "We're going to do whatever you feel like doing, Cassie. We didn't drive a thousand miles to sleep did we?"

Fifteen

~~~

SUNLIGHT GLITTERED OFF store windows as Dani and Cassie walked through the outdoor mall decorated with exotic flowers and bubbling fountains. Austin had settled himself in the center of the mall under a striped umbrella to eat a bowl of ice cream. "I'll catch up with you," he said.

"Don't you think that's beautiful?" Cassie asked as she stopped and stared into a store window.

Dani peered through the window of a bridal salon. A wedding dress of white satin, seed pearls, and delicate lace graced the front mannequin. "It's pretty all right, but do you suppose they make something in white denim for the bride-to-be?"

Cassie giggled. "That's the prettiest dress I've ever seen. Will you do something with me?" she asked, her eyes sparkling mischievously.

"Name it."

"Come inside, and *don't* laugh or giggle—just follow me."

"What are you going to do?"

Cassie took Dani's hand and dragged her toward the door. "Just play along."

"Cassie! No—"

As Cassie opened the door of the shop, a chime played "Here Comes the Bride." A saleswoman appeared and asked, "May I help you?"

Dani's heart pounded, and her mouth went dry. She heard Cassie answer, "My sister and I were admiring the dress in the window, and I was wondering if I could try it on."

The saleswoman eyed them for a moment, then beamed. "Oh, most certainly."

Dani swallowed hard.

"I'm Allison," the woman said. "Have a seat, and I'll show you our newest collection." She motioned them toward two lush peach-color velvet chairs. "Let me help you find the perfect dress for the biggest event of your life."

Dani could scarcely believe it. Was the woman

blind? Couldn't she tell that Cassie and she were kids out for a laugh?

Cassie sat, brushed her skirt, and said smoothly, "Thank you. I promised Mother I'd narrow the search, then bring her to see the dresses I like best."

The saleslady's back was turned, and Dani buried her face in her hands and groaned over the outrageous lie. Cassie gave her an elbow in the ribs. "A girl can't start too soon," Allison bubbled effusively. "When is the day, anyway?"

"The day?"

"Your wedding day."

Dani shifted helplessly in the chair, wishing the floor would swallow her. "It's in August," Cassie said with a straight face.

"These are the newest dresses for summer brides," Allison said. "White or candlelight?"

"Excuse me?"

"The color—are you thinking of pure white or off-white? Pale pink is also being shown. It's becoming increasingly popular with today's bride-to-be."

"Uh . . . white," Cassie said. "I'm into tradition."

"Traditional insanity," Dani muttered under her breath, hoping Cassie's strength would hold.

Cassie flashed a radiant smile at Allison as the saleswoman carefully carried several gowns over to them. "That one's still my favorite," she told her, pointing to a smaller size of the one in the window. "How do you know it's my size?"

"That's my job." Allison smiled. "Step into the dressing room, and I'll bet you a free satin pillow for your ring bearer that I'm right."

Cassie followed Allison into a dressing room, while Dani gripped the arms of the chair, planning an escape route for when the saleswoman figured out they'd been playing her for a patsy. Dani heard their murmured voices along with the soft rustle of satin as she gazed about the salon. There was gilt trim on peach-color walls; soft green carpet; charming clusters of dried flowers; a wall full of satin and grosgrain ribbons; a collection of silver, gold, and porcelain photo frames; and lush bouquets of silk floral arrangements mingled with white feathers and lace. The scent of roses and orange blossoms hung in the air. When Dani heard the door of the dressing room open, she straightened. Cassie came out smiling and asked, "So, what do you think, sis?"

Dani was overwhelmed by the vision of her sister. Cassie stood on a carpeted pedestal in front of a three-way mirror. The gown shimmered, and Cassie seemed to be glowing.

"Perfect!" Allison purred. "Didn't I tell you? You're a walkaway. That's what we call someone whom a dress fits perfectly, without need of alterations. I'll bet your fiancé will be absolutely speechless when he turns to see you walk down that aisle toward him."

Dani suddenly noticed the silk scarf wound around Cassie's head. It looked terribly out of place. As if Allison had noticed, too, she scurried over to another rack. "I have the perfect headpiece to complement that dress."

Dani couldn't take her eyes off her sister. She'd never seen Cassie look more beautiful. Her heart thumped as Allison held up a headpiece and fluffed the yards of white net. "If you'll remove the scarf, you might try this one," Allison said.

Removing the scarf meant showing Cassie's shorn hair, her chemo cut. Dani leapt to protect her sister. She couldn't allow the saleslady to ruin the moment by having a shocked expression. "My sister already has a headpiece, our mother's," Dani said almost too loudly.

"That's right," Cassie agreed. "My sister's going to be my maid of honor," she added as she eyed Dani gratefully.

Allison almost clapped her beautifully manicured hands together. "I have a stunning attendant's dress in summer green. Believe me, it would be lovely with your sister's red hair. What's your color scheme?"

"Green would be perfect," Cassie said.

Allison took out several dresses in various

shades of green, but highlighted one. Dani changed into the elegant gown and stepped up beside Cassie on the pedestal. Allison had pinned the bodice, and it fit her like a glove. The dress dipped off her shoulders, and her skin looked pale and creamy in the surrounding yellow light. Dani could scarcely believe her reflection in the mirror.

"Your coloring's so different, but you're both quite lovely," Allison said cheerily from behind them.

Cassie stared at herself in the mirror. The seed pearls gleamed and the satin shone. A fine net of intricate lace covered the dress's bodice and made Cassie's skin look like alabaster. Cassie's eyes trapped Dani's in the mirror and their gazes held. "I think we look fabulous," Cassie said, her eyes returning to her own reflection. "I feel like a princess."

"You both look like you stepped out of a fairy tale," Allison said. "Aren't weddings wonderful?"

An unbearable sadness stole over Dani as she realized that for Cassie there never would be a wedding day. No groom waiting at the altar. Nor attendants holding bouquets of flowers. Not ever. The magnificent wedding gown would forever be a fantasy. The Wish money easily could have been spent on giving Cassie a dream wedding. One that Cinderella would have envied. Now, what was left over after paying the enormous medical bills, would go to dress her family in mourning, and to bury her. Dani felt an involuntary shudder ripple through her.

"Are you cold?" Cassie asked.

"Just tired," Dani hedged. "We should go."

Cassie took one long, last lingering look at herself in the glass. "Will you cry at my wedding?"

"Yes."

Cassie's gaze caught Dani's in the mirror and she said, "Don't cry for me, Dani."

Dani searched her sister's face. Cassie looked wan and incredibly fragile. A film of tears blurred Dani's vision.

"I know just how you feel, my dear." Allison assured her. "It isn't easy losing a sister. But getting married is the natural order of things. People start new lives. It's inevitable."

The door chime played its tune, and the three of them turned to see a bewildered Austin at the front of the shop. Dani could imagine how silly they must look to him. Allison stepped forward. "The groom to be?" she asked.

Dani saw Austin's face redden, but he flashed a crooked smile. "The best man," he said, not taking his eyes off of Dani. "I go with the redhead."

Now it was Dani's turn to blush. Austin's eyes caught hers, and she felt her knees quiver. "We need to get home," Dani said abruptly.

Allison handed her a business card while Cassie went to change. "Please give this to your mother."

Dani took it. She noticed a silver picture frame, elaborately inlaid with flowers. She remembered that they'd wanted to buy a gift for their mother. The frame was beautiful and on impulse Dani told Allison she wanted it. "Of course, for the wedding portrait," Allison said with a bright, understanding smile. "A perfect choice. Your mother will be delighted."

Dani brushed past her and hurried to change, afraid she would lose control of herself. She was glad when the three of them left.

Back in their room, Dani felt exhausted and forlorn. She wished Cassie had never tried on the wedding dress. Dani was angry at herself. Why had she gone along with the play acting? It had only made the reality of her sister's situation more painful than ever.

Cassie stared moodily out the glass doors. "I would have been a great looking bride, wouldn't I?"

Dani's heart skipped. *Would have been*, Cassie had said. Did she know the truth about her condition? Dani had been so careful. "Of course, you'll be a terrific-looking bride," Dani said, ignoring Cassie's wording. "Let's hope there's some prince out there worthy of you."

Cassie smiled wistfully. "I'm going to walk down by the ocean," she said.

"Aren't you tired? Maybe you should rest for awhile."

"I'm tired all right, but I want to smell the sea now that I'm finally here."

Dani watched her through the doors until she settled on the sand. With a tired yawn, Dani stretched out on the bed and fell sound asleep. Hours later, when Austin woke her, she felt disoriented and drugged. "Come on, sleepyhead. It's time for supper," Austin said, shaking her gently.

"I'm not hungry."

"Well, I am."

Groggily, she sat up, rubbing her eyes. Dusk filled the room. "Where's Cassie?"

"She's still out on the beach, staring at the water."

Dani stumbled to the glass door to see Cassie sitting alone close to the shore where the waves were breaking. "That's what she was doing when I fell asleep. What's she been thinking about all afternoon? Come on—let's go get her." She hurried to her sister's side. "Want to go get some dinner? Austin and I are starving."

Cassie's knees were pulled up to her chest and her chin was resting on them. Her short hair fluttered in the breeze and Dani saw tears on her cheeks.

"Cassie what's wrong?"

"You know what's wrong." Cassie's voice was barely a whisper.

"No, I don't. Tell me."

Cassie turned. "Why didn't you tell me I'm dying?"

Sixteen

DANI FELT AN icy chill run through her. "What are you talking about?"

"Did you think I didn't know? Hadn't figured it out?"

Desperately, Dani tried to make Cassie feel better. "Oh, sis, the trip's been a downer. You're so tired—"

"Stop lying to me!" Cassie pressed her hands over her ears.

Austin crouched next to Cassie and turned her gently toward him. "Why don't you both come inside and talk."

"Someone should have told me, don't you think? Someone should have said something."

Tenderly, Austin hugged her as one might hug a small child. She clung to him, uttering soft, whimpering cries.

Dani felt numb. She thought about the half-truths they'd told and the outright lies. She realized she was just like her mother. She'd tried to protect Cassie from the awful truth. Dani felt disloyal to her sister, but sad that her choices were so awful. She didn't know what to say.

Austin broke the awkward silence. "I think you'd better call your mother."

The airport was crowded with tourists. Dani scanned the passengers coming through the door of the plane that had just arrived from Cincinnati, a sick feeling of apprehension knotting her stomach. When she had called, her mother had sounded hysterical, but once her mom had realized Dani and Cassie were all right, she'd calmed down and spoken in a deliberate authoritarian voice. "I'll be on the first flight I can get tomorrow morning," she'd said. Dani had given her their hotel phone number. "I'll call you back as soon as I can make arrangements. And when I get in tomorrow, Dani, you and I have plenty to discuss."

Dani had hardly slept. When morning had finally come, she'd discovered Cassie already out walking on the beach. Austin was sound asleep.

They had planned on going to the airport together, but right after breakfast, Cassie had been stricken with a headache. She'd insisted that Dani and Austin go on without her, and even though Dani had hated leaving her sister alone, she'd seen no way around the dilemma. She couldn't be in two places at once. Should she leave Cassie alone? What would happen if something went wrong? She had given Cassie a pain pill and gone with Austin.

Dani continued to fret until she saw her mother deplane. Surprisingly, Dr. Phillips was walking beside her. Her mother stopped short in front of her. She looked haggard and angry. Dani didn't know whether to hug her or not.

"Where's Cassie?" Mrs. Vanoy asked.

"Back at the hotel."

"You left her alone? You have absolutely no common sense."

Dani winced at her mother's words.

Dr. Phillips nodded hello to Dani and directed them, "Let's get our luggage and go."

As they rode in the van, no one made any attempt to talk. At the hotel, her mother swept into the room, dropped on the bed next to Cassie, and gathered her in her arms. "Oh, baby, are you okay?"

It was obvious that Cassie was in great pain. Still, she begged, "Don't be mad, Mama. I wanted to come so bad, and Dani knew it. Please, don't be mad at her."

Dr. Phillips quickly checked her and began asking questions. "Headache?"

"Bad one," Cassie mumbled. "I'd felt better. Yesterday. I really felt good, but now ..." She leaned back and moaned.

"I'll give you a shot." He drew clear liquid from a vial into a syringe and slid the needle into her arm. In minutes, the look of pain had eased from her face and she was asleep. Her mother leaned over, kissed her forehead, and tucked the blanket up around her chin.

The four of them went into Austin's adjoining room. Seeing the look of anger on her mother's face, Dani stepped out onto the patio for privacy. Her mother followed, leaving the door open.

"Do you have any idea of the hell you've put me through these past three days young lady?"

"Mom ... I'm really sorry. I never meant to hurt you, or endanger Cassie ... but ... it was something I *had* to do for her."

"I'm partly to blame, Mrs. Vanoy." Austin came out onto the patio. "Don't put all the blame on Dani."

Dani's mother turned on him. "I'm disappointed in you too, Austin. I thought you had better sense. Your parents don't know—I couldn't reach them, but just as soon as they get back in the States—"

"Mom, please . . . I practically forced Austin to help me."

"But why, Dani? Why didn't you come to me?"

"I tried to, but you wouldn't listen."

"When? You never said a word."

"Yes, I did . . . before she had her convulsion. But you were totally down on the idea of a vacation."

"A vacation!" her mother fairly exploded. "You call taking a critically ill girl hundreds of miles from her medical support system a *vacation*! And what's this craziness about One Last Wish and a huge check?"

Dani jutted her chin. "We both left you letters explaining everything—"

"I don't care what your letters said. You don't simply pull a girl in your sister's condition out of treatments and take off. What's the matter with you? Are you trying to kill her?"

Dani felt as if she'd been slapped. Dr. Phillips came to her defense. "Catherine, slow down," he insisted quietly. "We've talked about this. Unfortunately, the treatments weren't helping. Don't blame Dani."

"I was scared to death," her mother told Dani, pressing her hand to her mouth. "Don't you know how scared I was? How could you be so insensitive? You're old enough to understand."

Dani nodded, feeling tears brim in her eyes. "I was scared, Mom. I knew it would be hard on you, but what about Cassie? Every mile of the trip, I was so afraid." Dani ached to put it all into words. "After she told me about the One Last Wish letter, I decided I had to do something for her. That gave me the push to take the risk."

Dani cleared her throat before she went on. "Everything Cassie planned to do with her life was being taken away. Then JWC, whoever that is, wrote and said do something to make it better. Cassie wasn't strong enough to do it alone. I wanted to do something for her that would make her happy—something that would leave her with a wonderful memory. This was all I could think of. I didn't mean to hurt you, but I would do it all over again for her."

"You stubborn, foolish child! Where do you get the audacity to assume what's best for her? How can you take responsibility for her happiness? For her life? You could have killed her!"

"Mom, listen to me—Cassie *knows*."

"Knows what?"

"She knows that she's dying." Dani looked at Austin for moral support.

All the color left her mother's face. "You told her?"

"Mrs. Vanoy, Dani didn't have to tell her," Austin said. "Cassie just . . . *knows.* She told me that she's suspected it for a long time, but that she hasn't known how to deal with it. She said that the only reason she hasn't asked you is that you keep acting as if everything's going to be okay if she takes the treatments and keeps a positive outlook."

Austin stepped closer. "She's pretty scared, Mrs. Vanoy. Not only about dying but about leaving you and Dani. I think you need to talk to her about her condition—about dying. Not talking about it is tearing her up inside."

Dani was surprised by Austin's words to her mother. Last night, on the beach, after her initial revelation, Cassie hadn't said anything more to her about her feelings about dying, yet she'd talked to Austin. Dani felt dejected.

"She didn't want to say anything more to you about it, Dani." Austin's voice interrupted her thoughts. "I think she's angry because she feels out of control. I told her she needs to talk about it with you and your mother. There's nothing harder to face than the reality of death. Don't be upset, Dani. You can only do so much."

Dr. Phillips had been standing in the doorway. He walked over to Dani's mother and gently touched her shoulder.

"What should I do, Nathan?" Mrs. Vanoy asked, turning toward him. "I don't know what to do."

He gazed down at her tenderly. "I think you and Dani should ask Cassie what she wants to do. You've been a united family and faced tragedy before. You need each other, and Cassie needs you. But it's her life. Talk to Cassie."

Seventeen

Dr. Phillips continued talking to Dani's mother. Dani turned to Austin and pointed to the beach. She walked in the water where small breaking waves tumbled against the shore. Austin walked with her.

"I know you're angry," he said. "Don't be. We're on the same side, remember?"

Dani *was* mad. She knew she shouldn't be taking it out on Austin, but she felt as if she'd done everything possible to be there for Cassie, and had failed. "I had no idea that you'd become Cassie's confidant," she said hotly.

"You're her sister, and you sacrificed a lot to

make this trip with her. She didn't want to seem like an ingrate, and she knows that once this trip is over, you all have to go on living without her. For Cassie this journey is far more than a vacation, Dani. It's her last chance to feel normal, young and healthy."

She turned and faced him. "I don't want it to end," she said, her voice thick with emotion. "I don't want Mom to make us all go home."

"Maybe it won't end yet. Maybe your mother will have a change of heart."

"I doubt it."

"Dani, however it turns out, you did a fine thing for Cassie. Honestly, I'm glad I was a part of it. No matter how much trouble I'm in at home, I'm not sorry I drove you." Looking at him made her realize that there were many things about this trip she didn't want to end. Her feelings for Austin were such a jumble. She wished she could sort them out. She told herself she had no right to her feelings for him when everything else was such a mess.

"It's hot out here," she said suddenly, turning on her heel. "Cassie might be waking up soon. Let's go back."

Without a word, he fell into step alongside of her. Overhead, a cluster of gulls circled, their lonely cries echoing against the sky.

*   *   *

Cassie slept until the early evening. When she awoke, she was in high spirits, obviously feeling better. She hugged her mother and Dr. Phillips. "How did she talk you into coming along?" Cassie asked him.

"It's no secret—I'm more involved in your case than I ever intended to be. And you, your sister, and your mother mean a lot to me. Anyway, I had some vacation time coming. Dr. Sanchez is covering for me."

"I'm glad you're here," Cassie said. "Please help us keep Mom calm and convince her to stay and do something fun and normal."

Her mother busied herself folding clothes. For a moment, Mrs. Vanoy ignored the silence in the room as all eyes turned toward her. Finally, she tossed down a T-shirt and asked, "What? What's everyone staring at?"

"You heard Cassie. She wants to know if we can do something together," Dr. Phillips said.

"Yes. I heard her." Dani watched her mother walk stiffly over to the bed. "What would you like to do, Cassie?"

Cassie leaned forward eagerly. "I want to stay here for a few more days."

"But, Cassie—"

"We're here, aren't we? We'll never get this chance again. I want us all to be together. We have money to spend from the One Last Wish check, so that's not a problem—"

"About that money," their mother interrupted. "Tell me again exactly where this gift came from. I don't understand anything."

Cassie explained, with Dani's help, about the One Last Wish check. Dani handed over the letter that had come with the check. Their mother sat on the side of the bed and read it through. When she was finished, she folded it slowly. "JWC sounds like an extraordinary person. I can't imagine some stranger doing this. You have no idea who it is?"

"I've been dreaming about JWC. I think," Cassie whispered, "this person and I are on the same wavelength. I think JWC is a girl, a girl like me who's been in pain and feels helpless. A girl who knows what doing something special before the end can mean."

"What are you trying to tell me?" her mother asked.

"I mean to say that JWC understands what I feel. The money helped me—us—do something we'd have never attempted otherwise. It was a special gift, and I'm very grateful. And I'm especially grateful to Dani and Austin."

Mrs. Vanoy studied Cassie's face as she spoke. Then she said, "If we stayed"—Dani's heartbeat quickened—"what would you like to do?"

"I want to go to Disney World, just like my senior class."

Her mother looked dismayed. "But I don't think you're strong enough. The crowds—"

"We can get Cassie a wheelchair for the day, and there's a medical facility on-site should we need it. There's no reason we can't all go for a day," Dr. Phillips interjected quickly.

"We already have rooms." Austin added. "The doc can come in with me and you three can stay together."

"What do you say, Mom?" Dani asked.

Dani watched her mother's face. It seemed as if she were having a hard time making up her mind. Her mother looked at Dr. Phillips, then at Dani and Cassie. The lines around her mouth softened. "I say, let's go to Disney World."

"All right!" Dani cried, rushing to her mom and throwing her arms around her. Her mother hugged her back and Dani heard her ask, "Am I doing the right thing?"

From the moment they walked into the Magic Kingdom, Dani understood its name. In the sunlit center of the theme park, Cinderella's castle rose on lofty spires, fountains splashed jets of dancing water, bushes and hedges were clipped to resemble Disney characters. Snow White, Mickey Mouse, and Donald Duck danced in the streets.

Dr. Phillips settled Cassie in a wheelchair and tied balloons of every color to it. The wheelchair looked like a royal coach.

Mrs. Vanoy, Dani, and Austin walked along together, stopping to go on some of the relatively tame-looking rides. Dani and Austin rode on spinning teacups and some of the wild rides. Dani persuaded her mother and Dr. Phillips to go on Thunder Mountain. She, Cassie, and Austin sipped colas in the shade.

"You can do it, Mom," Dani insisted as her mother tried to convince everyone she was too old for such a ride.

"I think my doctor is crazy about our mother," Cassie told Dani when Austin had gone for french fries. She fiddled with one of the balloon strings with her good hand. "Would it bother you if they were more than friends?"

At first, Dani wanted to brush off the question. How would she feel? "I guess I'd be happy for Mom. She's been alone for a long time, but . . . but it would take some getting used to."

Cassie stared absently at the passing tourists. "Do you ever think about Daddy?"

"I don't remember him all that well."

"When he died, I thought I'd never stop crying. I missed him so much."

"I remember the day of his funeral. There were so many flowers. All these people I didn't even know kept coming up and saying things like, 'Poor little Dani and Cassie.'" Dani wadded up her napkin. "I didn't know what was going on. I remember feeling scared, though. I was afraid something might also happen to Mom."

"Me, too," Cassie confessed. "I thought that I might have to take care of you! Even though I was only eight, I told myself that I could raise you—be your 'Mommy.'"

Dani giggled. "What a chore that would have been."

"I could have handled it. Why, if I promised to read to you, you'd do anything I asked." The two of them laughed, then Cassie sighed. "After Daddy died, I used to talk to him at night when I was all alone."

"You did?"

"I really missed him. I hope I'll see him again." The wistful tone in Cassie's voice wasn't lost on Dani. "It's not as scary when I think about him waiting for me when I die," Cassie added.

Dani shivered. "I don't like talking about this," she said. "Here we are in Disney World, where everything's fun and everybody's supposed to be happy."

"I'm happy," Cassie told her. "I'm happier than I've been in months. And you and JWC made it happen. You're responsible for a miracle."

Dani felt warm inside. At least, she'd have her

sister's words to hold on to. "I wish I could stop time," she said. "That way, we could stay right here forever."

"Forever's a long time, Dani," Cassie replied. "Even if you spend it in the Magic Kingdom."

Eighteen

OF ALL THE attractions and rides in Disney World, the Haunted House caught up Dani's emotions. She sat with Austin, laughing at the fat, funny cartoonish impressions of ghosts that kept materializing out of the darkness throughout the ride. All at once, the car made a swooping revolution and swung them in front of a see-through panel that looked down on a spacious ballroom from a long-ago era.

On the floor below, beautiful ghostly couples whirled to the music of a haunting waltz played on illusory pianos. The gossamer figures floated serenely across the surface, spinning beneath crystal chandeliers lit by a thousand candles. Around and around they glided, on feet that never touched the floor, to music that never ended.

She could see the shimmer of the ladies' ball gowns, the flash of their jewels. She saw the stiffness of the gentlemen's formal frocks, the gleam of their shoe buckles. She knew that they were phantoms, form without substance, shadow without flesh.

"It's all illusion," Austin whispered. "They're holograms—you know, three-dimensional laser photographs."

The spectacle was unnerving. Her hands gripped the lap bar so tightly that her fingers hurt.

"Are you all right?" Austin asked as the car emerged from the tunnel of the Haunted House. His blue eyes narrowed, and a furrow creased his brow. "It wasn't real, Dani. It was only pretend."

"I know," she told him, trying to shake off the specter of the supernatural. "But it all looked so real." She wanted to tell him that in her imagination, she had seen not only the mystical illusion created by the wizardry of Disney, but the image of her sister and her father somehow entwined among the ghostly beings.

As they met up with the others, Dr. Phillips and her mother were settling Cassie in the wheelchair.

Cassie's eyes glowed, and she looked happy. "Wasn't that fabulous?" Cassie asked.

"Fabulous," Dani said, trying to regain her emotional equilibrium.

"Honestly, Dani," Cassie teased. "You look like you've seen a ghost!"

That night, back in their hotel rooms, they ordered pizza and talked about the fabulous time they'd had at Disney World. "Aren't you glad we went?" Dani asked her mother.

"Yes, I am, but please stop treating me like the grinch who stole Christmas. I'm glad we're all here together."

"That's the spirit," Dr. Phillips said, finishing his slice of pepperoni. "Now, what should we do tomorrow?"

"Tomorrow?" Mrs. Vanoy echoed. "I still haven't recovered from Thunder Mountain."

Everyone laughed. Dani eyed her sister, who had become very quiet. "Are you all right?" Dani asked Cassie quietly as she sat at the edge of her bed.

"I'm exhausted, I guess," Cassie answered, then closed her eyes and quickly fell asleep.

Much later, when everyone was asleep, Dani woke with a start. Her mother was still fast asleep. "Cassie? Do you want something? Are you up?"

Dani eased herself out of bed and felt her way

across the room. At the door, she caught hold of her sister. "What are you doing up?"

"Dani, I can't see clearly."

"It's just dark," Dani answered. "Why, I can barely see, either."

"Open the curtain, Dani. For me, the room is pitch-black. I think I'm blind."

Quickly, Dani pulled the cord that sent the curtain gliding over the track. Outside, the night was lit by a slowly sinking moon. Dani could make out the sand and the patio. "Can you see the patio?"

"I can't see anything." Cassie sounded frightened now.

"I'll turn on a light."

"No. Don't wake up Mom," Cassie insisted. "Please, take me outside."

Their mother heard their voices and sat up. "What's wrong?"

"Cassie wants to go outside," Dani answered.

"It's only five o'clock, honey. Wait till it's light," Mrs. Vanoy said as she walked toward her daughters.

"She can't see, Mom."

Their mother took Cassie's face between her hands. "Oh, baby . . . I'll get Nathan. Dani, put on the lights."

"No . . . wait," Cassie pleaded. "Let's the three of us go outside together."

Dani knew that Cassie's blindness meant that the tumor would shut down Cassie's vital organs and her capacity to function. She felt sick to her stomach.

Dani heard her sister's voice. "Mom, please— can't just the three of us go down to the water? I want to feel the sun come up. Then, if I have to go to the hospital, we'll go ..."

Her sentence trailed in the darkness, and all Dani could hear was the sound of her own breathing. "If that's what you want," her mother finally answered.

Dani slid open the door and felt the fresh, salty air. She heard the waves breaking on the shore in the distance. "My legs aren't working very well," Cassie said, sounding apologetic. "They're sort of numb."

"Mom and I can make a seat with our hands," Dani suggested quickly, and grasped her mother's wrists. Slowly, her mother grasped hers in return, so their hands formed a grid. Cassie eased onto it and wrapped her arms around their shoulders. They carried her to the water, lowered her onto the sand and sat down on either side of her, each holding one of her hands.

Dani felt the warm water wash over her feet and legs and soak the bottom of her nightshirt. She held her sister's hand tightly, afraid to let go, afraid that Cassie might wash out to sea, even though she knew that was impossible.

"I love the sea," Cassie said. "It sounds so wonderful."

"There is something comforting about it," Dani heard her mother say. She was surprised that her mom sounded so calm. "I'm glad you got to visit it. You wanted to so much."

"Then you aren't mad at us? At Dani for bringing me?"

"I was furious. Mostly scared that something would happen to you and I wouldn't be with you. But I'm all right now."

"Were you afraid I'd die?" Cassie asked. Dani heard her mother suck in her breath. "You should have leveled with me after the seizure," her sister went on. "I was so scared, I think what I imagined was worse than the truth."

"The truth?" Dani asked.

"That I was dying. It didn't take a genius to figure it out."

"I wanted you to have every chance, every hope possible," their mother explained.

"I want to know what's going to happen to me, I need to talk about everything," Cassie continued.

"You have some choices about whether or not to go on life-support machines," Dani said before her mother could stop her.

"No machines," Cassie said. "Let me die when my body says it's had enough."

"If you don't want the machines, you won't be put on them," her mother said in a voice that seemed controlled. "But the doctors can give you pain medication."

"That's good," Cassie agreed. "I don't want to hurt."

"We'll be by your side the whole time. We'll always be with you."

Cassie squeezed their hands. "I never thought you wouldn't be."

Dani struggled against cold, stark terror of what was to come as pink filled the horizon and the water lapped at her legs. Sandpipers, scurrying back and forth along the shoreline, seemed in such a hurry, but appeared to have no place to go.

"Is there anything you want us to do for you?" her mother asked.

"I wrote down what I want you to do for my funeral. It's in my old school notebook, in the van."

Dani had tossed the notebook in with Cassie's suitcase when she'd packed. At the time, she'd thought it would keep alive the illusion that Cassie could return to school after the trip.

"I'll do whatever you want."

"I picked some songs I'd like sung, and a poem I want read. I want to go back home, to the same cemetery where Daddy's buried. Can I be buried near him?"

"You'll have the plot I'd reserved for myself right next to him."

"You'd do that for me? Give me your plot?"

"I'd do anything for you."

"Let Austin's dad do the service. That will be comforting."

"If that's what you want."

"And I'd like you to bury me in my lace dress, the one with the puffy sleeves."

"You look so beautiful in that dress." Their mother's voice sounded soft, but full of tears.

"Is the sun up yet?" Cassie asked.

"Almost," Dani replied, watching it edge through a bank of clouds. "Maybe you can see it?" Dani hoped that Cassie's eyesight would magically return.

"I can feel it." Cassie turned her face heavenward. "It feels . . . warm."

A cry escaped from their mother's lips. She took Cassie in her arms, held her, rocked her. "I love you, baby. I wish I could die for you. I love you."

"I love you too, Mama."

Dani pressed her hand against her mouth. Cassie reached out for Dani and pulled her closer. "You'll have to be good to each other. I'll count on that so I won't have to worry." She paused, then said, "You can get Dr. Phillips now, Mom. I'm ready."

Nineteen

CASSIE INSISTED ON staying with Dani by the water while their mother ran to wake the others. Alone with her sister, Dani wiped her eyes. She wanted to be brave, like Cassie. The tears stung her eyes. "I don't want you to die," she sobbed. "I'm sorry I'm crying. I just don't know how you can face this."

"I don't want to die. But nobody gave me a vote." Cassie stretched out on the sand, balling her fists into its depths. "It feels so soft. Is the sun up all the way yet?"

Dani glanced seaward. "Not quite . . . just a little more."

"I'm sorry I couldn't see it one last time. But I'll never forget these past few days. I'll carry them here"—she touched her heart—"even if I'm locked up in some old hospital."

"Oh, Cassie." Dani continued to weep in spite of her best efforts to control herself.

"You have to be strong for Mom."

"But who's going to be strong for me?"

"Austin will be there for you. I like Austin, Dani. And he's crazy about you."

Dr. Phillips couldn't treat Cassie at the local hospital, but he arranged for her medical records to be sent from Ohio and acted in an advisory capacity to the doctor in charge.

Cassie drifted in and out of consciousness. Her mother called grandparents, friends, and other people back home. When Austin's parents returned from their mission work in Haiti, he explained the situation. Dani was glad they didn't bawl him out for taking their van on an unauthorized trip to Florida. It saddened her to realize that the next time she saw them, it would be at her sister's funeral.

Dr. Phillips made certain that Cassie's new doctor understood her wish that no extraordinary measures be used to keep her alive, so there was a minimum of equipment in her room. Dani, her mother, Austin and Dr. Phillips spent their days at the hospital staying with Cassie.

When the waiting became unbearable for Dani, she'd go back to the hotel room and run on the beach. If she ran at night, Austin ran with her. She concentrated on the beating of her heart, the pounding of her bare feet on the wet sand, the regularity of her breathing, the pumping of her arms. She found the exercise soothing.

"I'd rather play racquetball," she admitted to Austin after an especially long run. "Remember the day I beat you? It seems like a million years ago." They were walking back to the hotel, along a moonlit shoreline.

"I could probably find us a court," he told her, "if you really want to play."

She shook her head. "I don't want to be anyplace but here or at the hospital."

Dani mopped her brow with her hand. Perspiration dripped between her shoulders, and the air felt muggy and heavy in her lungs. A line of hotels stretched down the beachfront for as far as Dani could see, their windows sparkling with artificial lights. "I'll bet most people don't know what it feels like to watch and wait for someone die."

"JWC knows," Austin said. "Did you ever figure out who it is? Does your mother know?"

Dani shook her head. "It's a mystery to all of us. Cassie's convinced it's a girl, but I think it's a recluse who likes to do good deeds."

"No matter," Austin said. "Whoever it is understands about losing someone to death."

"Sometimes I wish it was all over for Cassie. I hate seeing her suffer. Then I feel guilty about wishing such a thing. Death is so final. Once Cassie's gone, she'll never come back."

"Maybe it would help to keep your perspective," Austin said.

"Perspective? What are you talking about? It's easy for you to say—someone you love isn't dying."

"Cassie's life was a gift, Dani. Just like the One Last Wish money. She didn't expect that money. She didn't ask for it. One day, some stranger with the initials JWC gave it to her. Unexpectedly."

The waves splashed against the shore. "We're grateful for the money. Without it, I'd have never had the courage to do this. We wouldn't be here if it wasn't for the money. Of course, Cassie didn't expect it."

"That's exactly the point," Austin said. He rested his hands on her shoulders. "Life is a gift, too. We don't get to choose if we'll be born. Or when, or who our parents will be. We just get to be alive. That's God's gift to us. *How* we live our lives is our gift to others. When a newborn baby dies, do you think it hurts his family any less because he was only a few days or even hours old?"

Dani shook her head. She understood completely what he was trying to say. "Grief doesn't have a life span, is that it?"

"That's it." He lifted her chin and looked deep into her eyes. "And neither does love. That's what JWC's letter was all about. Love is stronger than death, even though it can't stop death from happening. But no matter how hard death tries, it can't separate people from love. It can't take away our memories either. In the end, life is stronger than death."

The night wind blew the scent of salt through the air. Austin pulled her into his arms and rested his chin atop her head. "That's part of what faith is all about. We have to believe that every life has a purpose, no matter how long or how short it is. Your life has a purpose, too—to go on living, for those, like Cassie, who can't."

"I'm going to miss Cassie so much." Tears slid down Dani's cheeks.

"We're all in this together, Dani. You, your Mom, Dr. Phillips, me. That's the bonus. We don't have to go through this process by ourselves. I'm here for you whenever you want."

She clung to him until the moon rose in the starry sky and dimmed the artificial light from the high rises and condos. Together, hand in hand, they walked to the hotel.

*   *   *

The next morning, Cassie slipped into a coma. For two days Dani waited with her mother, Austin, and Dr. Phillips beside Cassie's bed. She measured time by the faces of the nurses changing shifts.

Cassie looked impossibly frail as she clung to life. Dani stroked her sister's new growth of downy soft hair. "I love you Cassie," she whispered.

At three o'clock on the third day, Cassie's breathing became short and shallow. Dani clutched her mother's hand as Cassie's breathing grew ragged, then staggered. Her chest stopped moving and slowly her body relaxed.

In the stillness of the room, Dr. Phillips put his stethoscope against Cassie's chest and listened. "She's gone," he said. Wordlessly, Dani wrapped herself in her mother's arms and together they clung to one another.

Twenty

"ARE YOU SURE you want to do this?" Dani's mother asked.

"Yes. Cassie would want us to—I know it," she said, trudging through the sand toward the place on the beach where a small crowd had gathered. Behind them, the sun was setting, and dusk was settling over the ocean.

Dani had decided she had to see the release of the loggerhead turtles. Cassie was the one who cared for marine life. Cassie would have been waiting on the beach. Austin understood why Dani wanted to do this. Her mother didn't, but still agreed to come.

Mrs. Vanoy sighed. "I'm not up to fighting the crowds. You and Austin rush ahead. Nathan and I will catch up."

Dani had begged to stay the extra two days for the release. "I want to go home," her mother had insisted through tears of grief. "We have to arrange for the funeral."

Dr. Phillips had come to Dani's rescue again. "Catherine, staying two more days won't make a single bit of difference. This is obviously important to Dani because of Cassie's wishes."

Her mother had agreed. Dani was grateful to Dr. Phillips, not only for taking up her cause about staying for the release, but for everything he'd done. He'd handled details about the death certificate and made arrangements with a local funeral home to fly Cassie's body back to Ohio. Dani realized he was in love with her mother. Cassie had been right about that.

"Come on," Austin said, taking her hand. "I see an open spot in the front."

"I didn't think so many people would come out for this," Dani commented.

"Who could have guessed dumping baby turtles on the seashore is such a big deal?" Austin led her around toward the ocean. Dani noticed several men and women in Florida park ranger uniforms, a couple of Jeeps, and a few policemen, who were telling the crowd to stand back and give the rangers room to work.

The rangers hauled large white buckets from the Jeeps and set them in the sand. "These turtle eggs were laid on this beach about two months ago," a ranger explained.

"We dug them up and took them to a hatchery for their own protection. A few days ago, they showed signs of hatching, and now it's time to release them back into the wild."

The crowd looked expectant. As the ranger continued his history of the turtles, Dani looked at the buckets. She could just see over the rim of one. It was packed with sand that kept wiggling.

". . . some of them weigh up to five hundred pounds and live to be a hundred years old," she heard the ranger say. "First, though, they have to get to the sea. And even if they make it through the line of predators on land, they have many to face in the ocean.

"But the biggest threat to these animals is man. Because we invade their habitat to build hotels and condos, the turtles have no place to nest. And when they do hatch, shoreline lights confuse them, and they turn toward parking lots instead of the sea, where they're killed by cars."

Dani felt sorry for the creatures, but couldn't help wondering how people could be so concerned about turtles when she'd just lost a sister.

Not an animal, but a flesh-and-blood human being whom she had loved. Whom she still loved.

"Here goes," she heard Austin say.

Dani watched as the ranger turned over one of
the buckets and began to smooth out the damp
sand. Suddenly, it seemed to come alive. A cluster
of small, dark turtles squiggled from the sand,
some still half stuck in leathery eggs the size of
Ping-Pong balls. The people watching murmured,
pointed, whispered in delight.

The tiny turtles crawled over one another,
sometimes turning each other over. The ones
stuck on their backs flailed frantically at the air.
Another bucket was overturned, and more baby
turtles scrambled upward. "Watch out for those
gulls!" a ranger called.

Dani looked up and saw a flock of gulls circling
overhead. One swooped down, seized a baby turtle and carried it away. Dani could see its small
legs twitching in the sky. "No!" she cried. The
bird had no right! It couldn't just take away this
little turtle that had been nurtured in the hatchery
and brought back to its home just before it had a
chance at life.

She broke from the group of people and yelled
at the overhead birds, throwing her arms upward,
forcing the gulls to veer away from the turtles
dashing to the sea. The crowd joined her, and

soon the beach was a melee of waving arms and shouts to scare away the birds.

Dani circled, all the time watching the swarm of newly hatched turtles tumble toward the water. Austin grabbed her shoulders. He was grinning. "Look what you started, you crazy girl!" he yelled.

She grinned back. "I did it for Cassie," she said. "Isn't it wonderful? We're saving them, Austin. We're saving the turtles. Wouldn't Cassie love it?"

She stopped, her eyes focused on one tiny turtle that had somehow managed to get turned around and was starting off in the wrong direction. Her heart thudded. Didn't it know that that way meant destruction?

She wanted to pick it up and set it back down in the proper direction. Before she could move, Austin caught her arm. "Wait," he told her.

"I want to help. I don't want it to get lost," she cried.

"Wait," he repeated. "Let it find its own way."

The baby turtle wandered in a zigzag pattern. Then it stopped and raised its tiny head. It was honing in on the moonlight, which cast a silvery path across the ocean to the line of the horizon. The turtle turned again, this time seaward. Dani grabbed hold of Austin's hand. "It knows," she said. "It knows the way home." Tears spilled down her cheeks.

They watched as the turtle scrambled forward and touched the edge of the warm water. A wave washed over it, caught it, and pulled it into the open arms of the sea. "She made it, Austin. The turtle made it."

Dani looked out at the rolling surf as her mother and Dr. Phillips came alongside of her and Austin. As they stood together, Dani felt Cassie's absence in one way, but her presence in another way.

She knew she couldn't have Cassie with her anymore, but she would always have her memories. She knew that just as the turtles were safe in the ocean, Cassie was safe in eternity. "We can leave now, Mom," Dani said. "We can go home."

ABOUT THE AUTHOR

LURLENE MCDANIEL has been a professional writer for more than twenty years and has written radio and television scripts, promotional and advertising copy, and a magazine column. She began writing inspirational novels about life-altering situations for children and young adults after one of her sons was diagnosed with juvenile diabetes. She lives in Chattanooga, Tennessee.

Lurlene McDaniel's popular Bantam Starfire books include: *Too Young to Die, Goodbye Doesn't Mean Forever, Somewhere Between Life and Death, Time to Let Go, Now I Lay Me Down to Sleep, When Happily Ever After Ends*, and the One Last Wish novel *A Time to Die*.